Kate sighed. Sweet April—here she is, afraid of losing Peter, and I'm telling her that I've found my man.

I'm an idiot for saying anything at all, but this was the worst time I could have told her how I feel. Her heart's breaking.

April rubbed her cheek on the pillow to wipe away her tears. "Matt fits in. It's like he's always been here. And that first night, he stood up for you even though he thought it would cost him his job. I wish Peter loved me like that."

I still think he does. The words were on the tip of Kate's tongue, but they wouldn't come out. Instead, she turned the conversation in a different direction. "Just a year ago, you and I were comforting Laurel about whether she'd ever marry Gabe. Back then, you said we had to have faith—that God wouldn't let us all be without husbands."

"He won't. He's already given Laurel Gabe, and it's looking like you and Matt are a good match. Maybe I'm supposed to be a spinster. I've been so busy telling God to give me a husband, I didn't ask if He wanted me to have one."

Aching silence filled the loft. Finally, Kate quietly admitted, "I've been doing the same thing."

Isn't that just like me, God? I'm always running full tilt at whatever catches my attention without thinking ahead. How many times have Daddy and Mama told me to stop and think? I've been so busy letting my head and heart rule me, I didn't seek Your will. I sort of figured since Matt is a good Christian, the soul part was taken care of.

April wiggled and rested her head on Kate's shoulder. "Remember what we alway

"You mean before we pr

In unison, they whispere

CATHY MARIE HAKE is a Southern California native who loves her work as a nurse and Lamaze teacher. She and her husband have a daughter, a son, and three dogs, so life is never dull or quiet. Cathy considers herself a sentimental packrat, collecting antiques and Hummel figurines. In spare moments, she reads, bargain hunts, and makes a huge mess with her new hobby of scrapbooking.

Books by Cathy Marie Hake

HEARTSONG PRESENTS

Don't miss out on any of our super romances. Write to us at the following address for information on our newest releases and club information.

Heartsong Presents Readers' Service
PO Box 721
Uhrichsville, OH 44683

Or visit www.heartsongpresents.com

No Buttons
or Beaux

Cathy Marie Hake

Heartsong Presents

To my dear friend, Deb Boone, who loves the Lord and others with every fiber of her being.

A note from the Author:
I love to hear from my readers! You may correspond with me by writing:

Cathy Marie Hake
Author Relations
PO Box 721
Uhrichsville, OH 44683
www.CathyMarieHake.com

ISBN 1-59310-868-0

NO BUTTONS OR BEAUX

All scripture quotations are taken from the King James Version of the Bible.

All of the characters and events in this book are fictitious. Any resemblance to actual persons, living or dead, or to actual events is purely coincidental.

Our mission is to publish and distribute inspirational products offering exceptional value and biblical encouragement to the masses.

PRINTED IN THE U.S.A.

one

Black smoke poured from the kitchen. "Oh, no!" April Chance ran through the doorway toward the oven, grabbing the corners of her apron to use as hot pads. The acrid smell of smoke nearly overpowered her. One quick yank, and the oven's cast-iron door clunked open. She pulled out two loaf pans and stared in dismay at the charred bricks inside them. Scalding heat burned through her apron. By the time she made her way back to the door, both hands were unbearably hot. Flinging the loaf pans, she squealed, "Ouch!"

"Ouch!" a deep voice echoed.

April waved one of her tingling hands to disperse the smoke. Peter MacPherson approached from barely a yard away. A big, black rectangle of soot marked the front of his faded golden shirt. "Oh, no! Peter, I'm sorry."

He reached out and encircled her wrists. Looking at her bright red fingertips, he frowned. "Let's soak yore hands straight away. Here. Sit down."

"I can't. I need to open the other door and make biscuits in a hurry. Otherwise, lunch will be ruined."

"You have yoreself a sit-down. I'll open the door and fetch you a bucket so's you cain cool off the burn." Somehow, Peter managed to make her sit on the back porch step. "Where's Kate? She cain fix the biscuits."

April shook her head. "No, she can't. She's in the barn, trying

5

her hardest to finish making her gifts for everyone. They're bound to be back in just a few more days."

"Then what about Greta?"

"She's over at her sister's for the next week or so."

"Makes sense. Betty Lou's got her hands full. Heard tell this was gonna be another set of twins. What will that make?"

"Seven children in five years." April didn't have to think about it for even a second. *All around me, girls I went to school with—some even younger—are marrying and having babies.*

Peter strode into the cabin, opened the far door, and pumped water into a mixing bowl. He returned to her side, set the bowl in her lap, and calmly slipped April's hands into the cool water. "There." He looked down at her, his red hair wind-ruffled and his blue eyes steady as always. A smile creased his face. "Ever' time I've come a-callin' this summer, the quiet here astounds me."

"It's odd, isn't it?" She looked around. Mama, Daddy, all four sets of her aunts and uncles, and the younger children had gone to Yosemite for a seven-week adventure.

"Yeah, but they'll all be back, noisy as always. Iff'n yore missin' the hullabaloo, you cain come o'er to my place. An hour there'll make you rush right home and hit yore knees to thank the Almighty for this peace and quiet."

April bowed her head and wiggled her stinging fingers in the water. "I don't think I'd ever feel that way. Nothing brings me more joy than being. . .surrounded. . .by. . .family." The last words came out choppily as she fought tears.

"Hey, there." Peter hunkered down in front of her. Cupping her jaw in his rough hands, he tilted her face up to his. "What's a-wrong?"

"Everything!"

He glanced over his shoulder at one of the loaf pans lying in the dirt. The huge lump of charcoal that was supposed to be bread rested beside it. "A coupla burnt loaves ain't worth yore tears, April."

"It's not just that."

"Hmm. Havin' a bad day all 'round?"

She nodded. "I broke a button off my boot this morning. Kate didn't rinse the laundry enough, so we're all rashy. I lost count while measuring the coffee. One pot was so strong, it could've dissolved a pitchfork, and the other was so weak, the boys said it tasted like bathwater."

Peter made a funny face. "How do they know what bathwater tastes like?"

April let out a feeble laugh that slid back into tears. "I've burned the bread, and I'm almost out of yeast. Then, I almost killed you by flinging the pans across the yard."

"Now I'm going to take offense at that." He sat down and bumped her shoulder with his in a friendly gesture. "D'you thank I'm such a weakling, a single loaf of bread would knock me into the hereafter?"

Staring at the mess, she tried to rein in her wild emotions. "It's more like a rock than a loaf!" Just then, her right wrist rested more heavily on the rim of the bowl so the water sloshed out and soaked her skirts. "Oh!"

"No use cryin' over spilt water. It'll dry." He wrapped his arm around her shoulder, and April soaked his shirt with her tears. "None of them thangs is 'nuff to upset you. Why don't you tell me what's a-really wrong?"

Embarrassed, she shook her head.

"Hey, it's just me. Peter. C'mon, little April."

"That's just it," she wailed. "I'm not little. I'm twenty-one, and I'm fat. Nobody wants me. I'll never have a family."

"Now hold on a minute, here."

Once the floodgate opened, she just kept talking. "Polly is a healer. Two years ago, she met Eric, and they got married.

Laurel is an artist. Last summer, when our group went to Yosemite—"

"She met Gabe," Peter said.

"And now they're married. I've been foolish enough to hope that since I was the next oldest Chance girl, this summer would be my turn. But it wasn't. It'll never be. Nobody wants a no-talent, fat girl."

"Nobody? No talent? Fat?" Peter half-pushed her away, then held her shoulders and gave her a gentle shake. "You stop right thar, April. God made someone extry special when He made you. You got a heart for servin' Him and carin' for ever'body 'round you. As for talent—there ain't a woman in ten counties who cooks like you do."

"And there's not a woman in those ten counties whose waist measures what mine does, either." Horrified she'd admitted that shameful fact, April lifted her soggy apron and buried her face in it.

Peter yanked the fabric back down and snapped, "I've never heard such nonsense. I could name off lots of women who got meat on their bones. There's not a man alive who won't admit that the quickest way to his heart is through his stomach. Jist like some folks like different dishes, men have different tastes in women. Me? I don't wanna find me a bride who's wasp-waisted. A healthy one like you—that's what I want. The bitty ones look like a wallopin' hug'll break 'em in half. Not that I want you to thank I'm bein' coarse," he added, "but a man has to keep an eye out for a woman who'll be by his side for years and years to come. He wants a wife who'll give him plenty of strappin' young'uns. Scrawny women wear out fast. With yore cousin and Aunt Lovejoy midwivin' as they do, you ken that's the truth."

Letting out a sigh, April tried to regain her composure. It didn't work. She muttered, "If everything you say about my cooking and size is true, then it's got to be me. There's something about me that scares men off."

"What'd make you say that?" His brows furrowed.

"Because it has to be the reason. I have to be the only girl in all of Reliable who's never had a boy walk her home from school or ask her to take a Sunday afternoon stroll." Confessing that only made her feel worse. April started to bolt, but Peter yanked her back down.

"Now jist you hold on." He gave her a stern look. "You best better get yore head screwed on front-wise. Starin' back niver got a body where she wanted to go."

April couldn't help smiling a little. Peter. Dear Peter. A girl couldn't have a better cousin. They'd grown up as neighbors, and he'd always been extra special to her. No matter how much schooling he and all of the other children on the MacPherson spread had, they only used proper English while in the classroom. The rest of the time, they fell back into the colorful dialect their parents had imported from Salt Lick Holler, Kentucky.

"Better. Much better," he crooned. "Iff'n you reflect on it a spell, you'll realize some important thangs. First off, Polly didn't want to accept none of the attentions of the local boys. Hit took Doc Walcott comin' from afar-off to grab her fancy."

"But Laurel had suitors coming out of the woodwork."

"True 'nuff, she did. But if you pause and recollect, they wasn't really carin' 'bout her. They wanted to have a pretty gal on their arm so's they could strut about like peacocks. 'Twas vanity what kept them sniffin' 'round her; not true and deep love."

"You can say whatever you want, Peter, but the truth still stands. Something's wrong with me. Never once has a boy even looked my way."

"No accountin' for the foolish ways of others."

"It's not them. It's *me*." The admission cost her all of her nerve.

"Not that I agree, 'cuz I don't. But let's grant for the sake of this here discussion that yore right and hit's you. How's about us workin' together on the problem?"

"What do you mean?"

"Well," he drawled, "case you niver noticed, I'm a man."

"Don't be silly. That's not the problem. The problem's that no one thinks I'm a woman."

"And so me bein' a man is the answer. I'll start shadowin' you and watchin' what yore doin'. Then we'll meet up, and I cain give you pointers on how to act. Yore gonna practice on me." He nodded. "Yup. That's what we'll do."

"I don't know. . . ."

He gave her a stern look. "Just how much do you want to be hitched and startin' a nest full of your own chicks?"

More than anyone knows. Biting her lip, April studied him. His eyes remained steady. "You'd do that for me?"

"Yup." He stood up and pulled her to her feet. "I reckon there's nothin' I wouldn't do for you. Starting with me holpin' you bake biscuits for lunch. What're we havin', anyway?"

৯

Up to his elbows in flour, Peter grinned at April. She sat across the table, her burned fingers slicked with butter. He'd applied the butter himself. It made for a good excuse to get to touch her—just like his noticing one of the pins holding her rich brown hair was sneaking free. He'd poked it back into place and relished just how soft her hair felt.

Chance Ranch usually buzzed with all of her aunts, her mother, and her cousin Kate, so he seldom managed to catch April alone. He'd been searching for an opportunity like this forever.

The Chance and MacPherson kids grew up calling each

other cousins. About a year and a half ago, when he realized he loved April, Peter sat back and thought matters through. His uncle had married April's aunt's sister. He and April weren't related at all. Some of his cousins just happened to be cousins to one of her cousins. Both clans were big and loving. Somehow, they'd taken one slender kinship tie and wrapped themselves together into one big family—but they really weren't related.

The plan he'd come up with out on the back porch nearly had him giddy. He'd been biding his time now for what felt like an eternity. Finally, he'd be with April and get her to see herself how he saw her. Once he did, he'd pop the question.

He tore his gaze from her and looked out the front window. Chance Ranch boasted a big yard in the middle of a sprawling rectangle of cabins and a stable. Each of the five Chance men had his own family cabin. Another cabin bunked the eight oldest boys, who now operated the horse ranch. Nestled protectively between the buildings was one more—the one April shared with her cousin Kate. If he had his way, Kate would soon be alone there, and he'd be building a place for himself and sweet April over on the MacPherson spread.

"Are you daydreaming?" April sounded astonished.

"Yeah, guess I've been gatherin' some wool." He couldn't wipe the grin off his face. "Don't believe I've ever seen you jist sittin' still. Even at the table, yore always hoppin' up to grab sommat."

April smiled at him. "I was just thinking the same thing about you—you're always in motion. Between minding the livestock and crops and herding all of your siblings and cousins, the only time I see you relax is in the pew at church."

"I reckon that's why they call Sunday 'the day of rest.'" He flopped another biscuit onto the pan. "I niver guessed cookin' was this much fun."

"I love being in the kitchen." Just as soon as the words came out of her mouth, April groaned.

"Whoa. Now that thar's one of them times I can spot straight off that yore sabotaging yourself. 'Stead of making a big to-do, worryin' about what you thank the feller is thankin' 'bout what you said, jist tack on another comment to string the conversation where you'd like it to meander."

"Like what?"

Peter looked at the biscuits in the pan, then the mess all over the worktable. "Mayhap you could said, 'Cookin' is loads of fun. 'Tis the cleanin' up that vexes me.' Then again, you could say, 'Don't you love how good a kitchen smells? I 'specially like bakin' on account of the way cinnamon and vanilla tickle my nose.' That sort of comment."

"I could do that!"

"Shore could." He grabbed the rolling pin and got ready to roll out the last bit of dough. Chuckling, he tilted the heavy utensil toward her. "Could be, you mention with all the knives and a rollin' pin, there's no safer place on earth for a woman. She's got herself a whole arsenal on hand."

April's laughter was ample reward for his nonsense. Peter sprinkled more flour on the table and started rolling the dough. "Next time someone sets a basket of biscuits afore me, I'm gonna have a new appreciation of them. You women make it all look so simple. Me? Some of my biscuits are thick and others are thin."

"You're doing great. When Gabe helped make biscuits the first time, he couldn't mix or roll them out. Laurel resorted to doing everything and just letting him cut them out with the glass. You're doing all of the steps on your own."

"I'm not 'zactly on my own. I've got you giving me directions." Peter glanced at her. "But what you jist did was good. A man niver tires of hearin' a word of praise."

"I don't want to be a liar, Peter. I can't tell somebody he's fabulous when he's just ordinary."

He halted. "Ain't nothing wrong with you appreciating how he pitches in and does the ordinary, April. Life jist flows along. Most days are much like the ones what came afore and the ones what'll come after. If you cain honestly tell a feller his daily effort is good, he cain walk back out and do the same work the next time with a warm feelin' in his heart."

Her brow furrowed. "I never thought of it that way."

"That's why you need me to holp you out. With me giving you a man's slant on matters, you'll understand what's important to us men." He emphasized his comment with a sage nod. "Yup. I'm gonna open them purdy sky-blue eyes of yourn and let you see thangs in a whole new light."

Lord, You ken I'm speakin' the gospel truth here. I aim to get my sweet little April to understand how special she is and how much I love her. Hit's kinda fun, like You and me are keepin' a pact all secret 'til we cain spring it as a big surprise.

"Peter?"

He raised his brows in silent inquiry.

"You won't tell anybody about this, will you?"

"About what?" Kate asked through the front screen door.

two

Peter scrambled to think of a way to steer the conversation so April wouldn't be embarrassed. "Kate, c'mon in."

"I can't. I've got stain all over my hands. Come open the door."

April started to rise.

"You jist sit yoreself back down." Peter strode to the screen and bumped it open with his elbow.

Kate's eyes grew enormous, and she started to giggle. "And I thought my hands were a mess! What are you doing covered in flour? Wait—first tell me what we're not going to tell anybody."

April turned redder than Ma's pickled beets.

Peter held his hands aloft. "I'm holpin' April make biscuits on account of she burned herself."

"You burned yourself?" Kate's nose crinkled. "What else did you burn?"

"You're a smart one, Katie Chance. You done figgered it out for yoreself." Peter gave April a look, then shrugged. "Couldn't keep it a secret."

"Couldn't keep what secret?" someone asked from the back door. That screen opened, and April's oldest brother, Caleb, tromped in. "And why are you feeding the birds and squirrels outta the dishes?"

April shot Peter a wry look. "And you thought it was quiet and peaceful around here?"

He grinned back at her. It hadn't taken much time for her to pull herself together. "I might have to reconsider that opinion."

Kate heaved a theatrical sigh. "Oh, well. Caleb knows now. Yes, April's decided to feed the birds and squirrels. With all of the younger kids gone, not as much food's been falling from the tables when we eat outside."

Peter chimed in, "And you know what a soft heart April has."

Her brother groaned. "I've heard everything now. It's not like it's the dead of winter and the animals are snowed in without a single scrap to eat." He scowled at the pans of unbaked biscuits on the table. "And why are you feeding them before you make our lunch?"

"Believe me, you'd never eat what I fed them," April said. "It'll only take twelve minutes for the biscuits to bake. During that time, you can both wash up."

"Now wait a minute," Kate said as Peter quickly shoved the biscuits into the oven. "I'm trying to decide which color to stain everything. Which sample do you like the best?"

Caleb walked over to scrutinize the scrap of leather she held out. Peter gave April a sly wink as he passed her and went to give his opinion.

"The darkest brown is best for the men's belts," Caleb said.

"I agree." Still staring at the leather, Peter asked Kate, "What else are you making?"

"Knife sheaths for the boys and leather cases to hold the women's hair pins and jewelry."

"You've got five colors there," Peter observed. "Why don't you stain each of the cases a different color?"

"Do all the knife sheaths in this shade." Caleb jabbed the middle color. He then stared at Peter's chest. "What happened to your shirt?"

"I was helping April feed the birds and squirrels." Peter shrugged and said in a bland tone, "I stopped her from tossing the food too far away."

Kate lit the lantern and set it on her workbench. Since April had burned her hands, she couldn't very well wash dishes or cook today. Already feeling pressed for time, Kate had still stopped working on the gifts and pitched in. She'd never been one to wake up early, so staying up late to work suited her fine.

Frowning at the table, she tried to position the lantern so the leather pieces wouldn't be in shadow. Staining leather evenly took concentration and a careful touch. Attempting to do it in poor lighting guaranteed spots and streaks.

"Need another lamp?" Tobias asked.

Kate didn't even turn around at the sound of her oldest brother's question. "Yes, thank you. I want to get these done. I'm afraid everyone will come home before I do."

Tobias lit another lantern and hung it on a bent nail. He sat and whittled as she started to stain a box. "How badly burned are April's fingers?"

"Not horrible, but not good. In about a week, she'll be back to the stove."

"Good thing," he chuckled. "If us boys have to start taking a turn at cooking, the chow's liable to turn out as tough as that leather you're working on."

Capturing her lower lip between her teeth, Kate concentrated on keeping the stain even. She'd started on the lightest one first, then would work her way clear down to the darkest color. That meant if she stayed up late, she might get three boxes and all of the sheaths stained tonight. That would leave two boxes and five belts for tomorrow.

"I've lost track of what day it is," she said.

"Wednesday. No, Thursday."

She laughed. "You don't sound any more sure than I am."

"Well, I'm trying to figure it out. We had church Sunday.

Monday, we took delivery on the stallion. Tuesday, Tanner nearly got himself trampled by that horse. Yesterday, I had supper at Lucinda's."

"You're pretty sweet on her. Are you getting serious?"

"Can't say." He set down the clothespin he'd whittled on the edge of her workbench and started on another.

"Can't, or won't?"

"Don't be so pushy, Kate. It's none of your business unless I announce I'm planning to marry."

She shot him a saucy grin. "By then, it'll be too late for me to register any objections."

"Nothing objectionable about Lucinda." He shaved off a corner of the rectangular block of wood.

"It all depends on where you stand as to what you see." Kate rubbed one last spot on the box, then set it aside.

"Just what was that supposed to mean?"

Capping the lid on one can of stain and opening another, Kate mused, "Ever notice how Lucinda won't say much to any of our aunts or me?"

"Can't say as I have." He glowered at her. "She's polite as can be to Mom."

"Exactly. But only to Mama. If Lucinda were shy, I'd under—stand, but she's not. At first, I thought maybe it was me—that she thought my stained hands were dirty or something. And when she's been here for meals, it's cute how the two of you manage to sit side by side. But Tobias, she doesn't ever come in to help in the kitchen. She hasn't offered to clear the table or do dishes." Kate shot her brother a quick glance.

His brows were furrowed, but he continued to whittle. "When she's here, she's a guest."

"Maybe the first time or two. But the newness wears off."

"There are seven women in the kitchen. You don't need Lucinda."

"Aunt Lovejoy's back pains her too much to do any appreciable work, but she still sits there and enjoys our company and conversation." Kate knew she was treading on sensitive ground, but someone had to say something. Her brother needed to face the fact that Lucinda wasn't a good match for him. "Since everyone left, and April and I are doing all the women's work, a little help is in order."

"Is that what this is all about? You're feeling put upon, so Lucinda is to take the blame?"

Laughter bubbled out of her. "When have I ever been afraid of pitching in and working?"

"You're a Chance. Not a one of us could be lazy if we tried." His eyes narrowed as he rounded the end of the clothespin. "As for Lucinda spending time in the kitchen when everyone else is in Yosemite—she doesn't have all that much in common with either April or you."

"No, she doesn't." Kate dipped the corner of a fresh rag into the stain and started on the next box. "You might want to think about that. We're the same age, but Lucinda hasn't ever done a single chore. Maybe you need to start watching her. She's got a lively way about her and quick wit. Those qualities and being pretty make it easy for her to turn a man's head. I'm saying you might look at her from a different perspective."

"You wouldn't have brought it up unless something was weighing on your mind." His hands continued to move the knife across the wood in steady, sure strokes. "So why don't you go ahead and say what you intend to, instead of sidestepping all over the place?"

Kate took a steadying breath, then said, "Lucinda's mother orders her expensive gowns from back East. Their family has a cook, and servants do her laundry. Would someone like that survive on Chance Ranch?"

"She could learn how to cook and such."

"Yes, she could. But does she want to?"

Tobias snorted. "If we do marry, she'd have to."

"Not necessarily. I mean, you're right—she would. But I don't think she believes that."

"Why wouldn't she? Lucinda's been here a lot. She knows Chance women pitch in and do whatever needs doing."

Kate shook her head. "Everyone in Reliable knows Mama received a sizable inheritance. Don't get me wrong, Tobias. I think you're quite a catch, but I wonder if Lucinda thinks that if you and she get married, there's plenty of money to hire a housekeeper and cook so she won't have to work."

"You're reading far too much into this."

"You could be right." Carefully rubbing the leather so the stain worked its way into the floral pattern she'd impressed into it, Kate couldn't hold back one last comment. "When the time comes for any of us to marry, I'm hoping and praying we'll all be blessed like our parents. Regardless of how much or how little money they had, they've given their hearts to this family and been true helpmeets. A woman who worries more about keeping her hands soft than about standing by her man isn't cut out for ranch living."

"Sis, you're not exactly the person to dish out advice. You're only a year younger, but you have yet to even think about the future."

His words cut her deeply. "Who says I haven't?"

"Look at yourself." He waved his hand at her from head to toe. "Half of the time, I'm not sure you even bothered to brush your hair that day, and you're still tromping around in men's boots."

"Are you ashamed of me?"

"Don't go putting words in my mouth."

Not fooled by his evasive answer, Kate rubbed the stain in harder and faster. She dipped the cloth into the stain again and spread it with every scrap of concentration she could muster. Even then, she couldn't wipe away the painful knowledge that her big brother considered her a disgrace.

She finished that box and the next, then set to staining the knife sheaths. Six of them to do. . .five. . .four. . .three. Suddenly, each sheath represented how males dominated Chance Ranch. In her own generation alone, fourteen boys still lived here; with just her and Kate left, the girls were vastly outnumbered.

Two. Two sheaths for the very youngest Chance boys. Those boys would be allowed to run wild, get filthy, and holler to their hearts' content. No one would bat an eye at such behavior. No one would comment if a man's hair was a mess or inspect what he had on his feet.

"You're riled," Tobias said as he set his third clothespin on the worktable.

Kate bowed her head over the sheath and rubbed more furiously.

Tobias whistled. "*Hoo-ooo-ey*. You're so hot, it's a marvel there's not steam rising from the table."

Never in all of her hours of doing intricate leatherwork had she toiled so intently. *One more. I only have to stain this last one. Then I can walk away.*

"Sis." Tobias had the unmitigated gall to sound concerned. "Listen—"

Kate shook her head. "You've already said plenty tonight. I don't want to hear another thing from you."

"Aw, for cryin' in a bucket. How is it that you work leather like a man, gallop around like a hoyden, and suddenly get your nose out of joint because someone points out that you're not the picture of femininity?"

"My being a woman didn't stop you from asking me to repair your saddle last week."

"I knew it. I knew when you got all silent that I'd tweaked your pride."

She finished the last knife sheath, capped the stain, and tried to get the worst of the brown splotches off her hands with turpentine. *Why bother? I'll get them even darker when I finish staining the rest of the stuff tomorrow.*

Avoiding looking at her brother, Kate mumbled, "I'll see you in the morning."

Tobias reached out and grabbed her wrist. "You're not walking away yet. Ephesians 4:26."

"Be ye angry and sin not: let not the sun go down upon your wrath," she quoted. The verse had been drilled into all of them. There were times when two or three family members sat up a good portion of the night before settling an issue, but they didn't climb into bed until the matter was resolved.

He jerked his chin toward a stool, then turned loose of her.

Kate backed up a step. "I'm not angry. I'm hurt."

"Leave it to you to start acting like a woman about this. Everything else, you behave like a—"

"Like a what?" She folded her arms across her chest.

Tobias compressed his lips.

"I know what I am. I'm a woman. You might not think leatherwork is feminine, but it's what I do. It helps our ranch. It's never kept me away from doing my share of gardening, minding the younger kids, or washing piles of laundry. I mended that shirt you're wearing, and I made the supper you ate tonight. Tomorrow, I'll milk the cow, gather the eggs, and make your breakfast. Doing those things makes me happy because I love our family. Knowing you're ashamed of me—it hurts. A lot. I have hopes and dreams for the future. Know this, though: Any man who can't see past some stain on my hands isn't the type I want to marry."

three

"Are you sure you'll be all right?" April stood out in the yard and studied Kate's face. She and her cousin shared a cabin. When Kate had crawled into bed the previous night, she'd been utterly silent. Usually, they'd chatter awhile up in their beds in the loft, but Kate had turned her back and pulled the covers over her head. This morning, Kate barely spoke a word.

"Of course I'll be okay." Kate made a shooing motion. "We need you to buy essentials before our mothers get home. They'll have a fit if we're out of anything."

"I could give Peter a list."

"Kate'll be fine." Tobias stepped up beside Kate and rested his hand on her shoulder. "We all love her chili. Tanner and I'll do the lunch dishes so she can finish staining the gifts."

"I'm using the very last of the yeast to bake bread. Don't forget to get more," Kate said.

"Then we're off." Peter curled his hands around April's waist and lifted her onto the buckboard. He rounded the front, gave each of the horses an affectionate pat, then climbed up. As he sat on the bench beside her, April tried to scoot over to give him a little more room. *Why do I have to be six axe handles wide?*

"You fixin' to fall out, first bump we hit?" Peter gave her a meaningful look. A sly smile lifted his lips as he tilted his head toward his left. "C'mon over here."

"See you later," Kate said over her shoulder as she went back into the house.

"Giddyup." Peter flicked the reins, and the buckboard

started to move. Four crates and a pair of bushel baskets full of produce rattled in the back.

"It's uncommon for you to make a trip to town. Usually the MacPherson women go."

After glancing both directions, Peter looked back at her and winked. "Gotta make shore nobody's close 'nuff to hear us. Goin' to town made for a good excuse. You and me are gonna start in on our plan. I reckon this'll give us a time to start practicing."

"So what do I do?"

"Well, a buck don't want his gal perched so far away."

April said, "I scooted closer back home."

Peter chuckled. "You wiggled a mite, but if you got any closer to me, 'twas only a speck. 'Stead of actin' like I'm fixin' to bite you, you oughtta be close 'nuff for me to catch a whiff so's I cain 'preciate yore perfume."

"I don't wear perfume."

He thumbed back the brim of his hat and shook his head. "When I hefted you into the buckboard, I caught somethin' that smelled sweet."

Hefted? How mortifying. That's what he thinks?

"That's a right fetchin' shade of pink yore goin'. Hit's down-right cute. Ain't nothin' a-wrong with a feller likin' his ladylove's scent."

"It's just the soap Polly makes for me."

"Iff'n she cain make it a soap, I'm shore she could make it into a perfume or lotion, too. Whilst we're in town, you cain drop in and ask her. You need to make it a habit to be dabbin' some on each day. A gal niver knows 'zactly when her beau might take a mind to drop in."

April nodded glumly. *No man's ever going to get close enough for perfume to matter. Peter's one of the strongest men around, and he has to "heft" me up.*

Coaxing the horses to take the right fork in the road, he said, "Speaking of lotion, I'm countin' on you to remind me to get some of that lotion my ma's taken a shine to."

"Jergens. Aunt Lois likes Jergens. Aunt Eunice favors making her own concoction of Vaseline and mineral oil."

"Wish she wouldn't. It rubs off on ever'thang. Stuff's slicker'n spit on a glass doorknob."

April managed to laugh.

Peter smiled at her. "Now that was real good of you. Knowin' his gal thinks he's clever makes a man right proud. And you knowin' the likes and particulars of my kin—that tells me you care 'bout those I love. A feller wants his bride and family to get on real well."

"Of course, I love you all. The Chances and MacPhersons are like one big, happy family."

"Ain't that the beatenist thang? I always thought you were kin, but yore really not. Thank on it a spell. Yore aunt Lovejoy is Polly's stepmama. Since my aunt Tempy is Lovejoy's sis, that means Polly is a cousin by marriage to all of Tempy and Mike's children."

April's eyes widened. "I never gave it any thought."

"But 'tis the plain truth."

"I don't want it to be, though." April sighed. "I love all of you MacPhersons."

"Glad to know it."

She perked up. "Lovejoy says family's made by opening our hearts to others, not just by blood alone. I'm going to adopt you all."

"You shore you know what yore askin'?"

April laughed. "I most certainly do. My mind's made up."

When they reached town, Peter stopped in front of White's Mercantile. "Wait right here a moment," he ordered.

April sat up on the bench seat and stared down at her

hands. They looked ugly. Blisters swelled on the pads of all ten fingers.

"Howdy, Mrs. White. I brung in fresh truck."

"Lovely!" the storekeeper said from the doorway. "I've been desperate for some."

Peter lifted the heavy crates and carried them inside. Farm work resulted in his strength—*strength he has to use to "heft" me.* April pretended to look back down at her hands.

"We'll be back in a bit, ma'am. We're gonna go pay our respects 'cross the street."

"I'll tally everything up and put it out to display." Mrs. White bustled back inside the mercantile.

April stood up and was ready to jump down.

"You hold it right thar," Peter boomed. "You tryin' to break an ankle atop already havin' burnt hands?"

"I. . .um. . ." *Don't want to break your back.*

"What's this about burned hands?" Eric Walcott asked as he stepped out of his office directly across the street.

"Howdy, Doc." Peter clamped his hands around April and swept her down. "April sorta burnt her hands yesternoon. Long as we're in town, seems like a good notion to have you take a look-see."

"Sure. Come on in."

Peter steered her across the street, up the steps, and into the office.

"Really, I'm fine."

"I'll be the judge of that." Eric took her by the wrists and turned her hands palm upward. "The blisters have to be tender. I don't want you to pop them, though. It invites infection."

"Got a salve for her?" Peter asked.

"That's not necessary." April pulled her hands back.

"Actually, I prefer burns of this nature to be kept clean and dry."

"Burns of what nature?" Polly walked in, cradling her daughter.

"April burnt her hands," Peter said.

"They're fussing over nothing." April walked over to her cousin. "How's our pretty little Ginny Mae?"

Peter stepped up and swiped the baby just before April took hold of her. "Yore in no shape to be totin' a young'un." He expertly popped the baby up by his shoulder and took to rocking her side-to-side.

"She's got a new trick," Polly said. "This week, Ginny Mae decided to sit up all on her own."

"She's bright-eyed as a bushy-tailed squirrel," Peter announced. "Polly, April's gonna need lotion for her hands. Cain you make her some?"

"I'll get on it right away."

"We're gonna go yonder to White's. We'll drop back in afore we hie home."

Steps sounded on the boardwalk. Someone entered the office. "Doc? I got me a carbuncle on my leg. Tried a drawing salve on it, but I'm hurting."

To April's surprise, Peter swiped a small towel, draped it over his shoulder, and switched Ginny Mae to that side. He patted the baby on the back as he said to Polly, "Looks like you and yore man got yore hands full. April and me—we'll carry little Ginny Mae on over to the mercantile with us."

"There aren't many men I'd trust with my baby," Polly started rolling up her sleeves. "But I've seen you with so many little ones in your arms, you probably have more experience than I do."

"Comes from bein' one of the eldest." Peter gazed down at Ginny Mae and smiled as he tenderly toyed with her darling baby curls. All told, the three MacPherson brothers had fathered thirty-four children. Twenty-five survived. "From the time I was knee-high to a grasshopper, I was holdin' or changin' a wee one."

"I'll hold her." April reached over.

Peter turned sideways so the baby was too far away for her to snag. "Nope. I'm gonna be stubborn here. Yore hands are tender. Not only that, but with Ginny Mae bein' the first Chance girl in twenty years, you all hog her to yoreselves. Hit's finally my turn to tote her, and that's that."

"Do you need anything from the mercantile?" April tore her gaze away from the sweet sight of a big, strong man doting over a bitty baby girl and looked at Polly.

"I went there earlier this morning."

"All right, then. Let's get outta their way." Peter took a step, then halted. "Polly? You gonna make that lotion smell good?"

Laughter bubbled out of Polly. "You still haven't forgiven me for using McLeans Volcanic Oil Liniment on you?"

"Truth be told, I'd ruther tangle with a skunk than have you put that on me again. I've forgiven you, but I ain't forgot. 'Twould be a cryin' shame for you to make little April sommat even a portion that stinky."

"I'll use calendula. It soothes skin and smells nice." Polly smiled. "I planned to make you more soap, April, but I've been busy."

"Don't push yourself," April said. "I still have almost a whole bar." As Peter walked her across the street, April fretted, "I should have brought food for Polly."

"This here babe is six months old. Polly's got her feet back on the ground."

April stopped and gave him a telling look.

Peter threw back his head and let out a belly laugh. Eyes twinkling, he leaned down and murmured, "I've suffered a few bellyaches from Polly's cookin'. I reckon she's given up and buys plenty of them fancy, canned vittles."

Shuddering, April whispered back, "She does."

"She and Doc look happy 'nuff." Peter took her arm and pulled her across the street. "Fact is, we et some of them canned vittles when we went to Yosemite last summer. Ever' last meal you made tasted grand. What you need to do is make shore when li'l Ginny Mae here comes to an age where she cain stand afore the stove, you teach her. Come the day she marries up, her man's gonna thank you from the bottom of his heart."

"Are you sure it won't be from the bottom of his stomach?"

Peter grinned. "April, I truly like that 'bout you. You've got yoreself a quick mind, but you niver speak words that cut."

April blinked.

"Now yore supposed to thank a buck when he pays you a compliment."

"Thank you," she said.

"Welcome." Peter continued to hold Ginny Mae against his shoulder as easily as could be and opened the door to the mercantile. When the bell rang, the baby let out a wail. "Now, don't you be cloudin' up and fixin' to rain." Peter shifted Ginny Mae and kissed her.

"Hello," Mrs. White called over from the produce display. Her face suddenly wrinkled in concern. "I didn't realize you'd brought in your aunt Tempy's baby! Oh, dear. And you went to see Doc. If you brought the baby, Tempy must be bad off and—"

"No, no," April hurriedly said. "It's Polly's little girl."

"All my kin are hale as horses." Peter turned so Mrs. White could see Ginny Mae. "Doc and Polly are busy, so we took the prize and ran."

Mrs. White let out a tense laugh. "You had me worried for a moment there."

Ginny Mae continued to fuss. April said, "Not many men would call a noisy baby a prize."

"As I said yesternoon, no accountin' for the foolish ways of others."

"I can hold her," April offered as she reached for Ginny Mae.

"Not with burnt hands, you won't. Grab us up one of them baskets. I'll tote it about whilst you fill it up with the stuff we need."

Mrs. White popped a cabbage onto the top of a pretty row. "If you brought a list, I could fill it for you."

April said, "Kate told me to ask if the rivets she wanted have arrived."

"I'll take a look in the back room. There's a crate of things I haven't unpacked yet."

"Thanks."

Peter rhythmically patted Ginny Mae. "We'll rustle up whate'er we need out here. April, how's about you fetching the basket?"

"The first thing we're getting is the Jergens for your mother."

"Gladdens me that you remembered." He followed her and swiped the basket she'd tried to hold. "Some of that Johnson & Johnson talc could help a bit if the lot of you are still rashy."

April's jaw dropped.

"Hot as it's been, might as well get a canister for you and Kate to share in your cabin and another for the boys." Calm as you please, he stood there, waiting for her to fill the basket.

She grabbed a canister of talc and the lotion, then shoved them into the basket.

Peter leaned down and stared her in the eye. "I ain't a-gonna budge from this spot 'til you get the boys some talc. Tanner was itchin' to beat the band at lunch yesterday."

April wanted to tell him the talc was for the boys, but she'd be lying. It was only merciful to get another. Putting a second one in the basket, she said brightly, "So what next?"

four

"Johnna asked me to bring home some Mum."

Her face went burning hot. *Horses sweat, men perspire, women glow.* Her mother, having been a missionary who grew up wearing all of the proper clothing a true lady wore even in the brutal heat of the Hawaiian Islands, had quoted that phrase more than a few times. Buying a deodorant practically announced to all and sundry that a woman sweated like a draft horse.

Peter grinned. "C'mon, April. After we went camping in Yosemite last year, you spoilt ordinary livin' for us, totin' along all those extry little thangs."

"Like what?" She hoped to distract him from the fact that she was slipping two packages of Mum deodorant into the basket.

"Ulysses and me—we got the whole clan using Sheffield's Crème Dentifrice now 'stead of just dippin' into a box of bakin' soda. Ma's happy as a dog with two tails over it. That tube the cream comes in is right nifty, and we ain't swiping stuff from the kitchen that the womenfolk were countin' on."

"I'm surprised. I thought you were going to say you got started using Ivory soap, but Gabriel is the one who brought that to camp."

"Now that you mention it, I probably oughtta get a bar. Doc and Polly recommended Aunt Tempy use it on baby Artemis."

"The rivets are here," Mrs. White called out. "And Peter? Your mother and aunts always make new outfits for the kids

30

to wear to school. Do they need anything? Buttons? Thread?"

"Yes, ma'am. The women shore have been stitchin' a heap to make all the little ones new duds. Thankee for remindin' me. They need more thread."

April walked over to the next aisle and reached for the gold. She didn't need to ask about the color. The entire MacPherson family wore golden yellow. Years back, Peter's uncles made that decision, and they'd stuck with it for the past decade. Once they determined to do something, the MacPherson men didn't waver in the least. "One spool or two?"

"Two. Iff'n they don't need two now, 'twon't go to waste in the future."

They moseyed around the store, filling the basket with embroidery floss, Semple's chewing gum, cinnamon, and salt. "How's about boot laces? I broke mine this mornin' and tied it together. Twine's a pain in the neck. Knots up and won't let go, so a body has to lace in a new length each day."

"Why don't you have Kate make you leather ones? She does it for all the Chance men."

"I hate botherin' her."

"Nonsense." April breezed by the laces and toward the ice box against the far wall. "I need to get some yeast."

"Best you toss in a few cakes of that Fleischmann's for us, too. With Tempy just birthin' Artemis, the women haven't been to town in a few weeks. I'm guessin' they're runnin' low and jist didn't thank to ask me to stock up."

"I'm taking all of the yeast, Mrs. White. Will that be a problem?"

"No, I'm due to get a new shipment in tomorrow at the latest. Peter, I ordered the sugar your mother said she wanted for canning. It'll be in day after tomorrow."

"Obliged."

"It's always fun to see what comes in." Mrs. White fussed

with her lace collar. "You'd think they'd be accustomed to me asking for all of the bags to be yellow after making that request for years on end."

"I didn't get too excited last year. Most all of the sacks had posies all o'er 'em." Peter grimaced. "Hit took Ulysses and me two whole days to talk the women outta stitchin' us men shirts from that girly fabric."

"It's a shame it wasn't here for you today."

"I'm enjoyin' the trip to town. Mayhap in a day or two, me and April will come back to pick up the sacks."

Putting the yeast on the counter, April looked at the contents of the basket and the small packet of rivets. "What a shame that the sugar hasn't arrived. It's hard to imagine we made a trip to town for such a paltry collection of things."

"Thangs don't have to be big to be important." Peter lowered Ginny Mae onto the counter and grinned as she teetered a little before managing to sit up. "Do they, l'il darlin'?"

"Will there be anything else?" Mrs. White asked.

"I'd like three yards of yellow flannel, please."

"What is she doin', getting yeller?" Peter asked the baby, who promptly drooled all over the arm he used to steady her. "Don't she ken the yeller's for the MacPhersons?"

"I sure do." April smiled. "I thought I'd make a few gowns for Artemis."

"Now ain't that sweet."

Mrs. White took the new bolt from the shelf and started to unroll it. Clucking her tongue, she frowned at the fabric. "Shameful. Just shameful. Look at that." She unrolled more. "This flaw goes down the middle of the whole bolt!"

"Wouldn't be seen on a gallopin' goose," Peter said.

April leaned forward. Carefully inspecting the flaw, she said, "I could work around this."

"I can't charge you full price for spoiled goods. How about if you buy four yards and I sell it to you, two yards for a penny?"

❧

After storing their purchases in the bed of the buckboard, Peter led April back into Polly and Doc's place. "Got yoreself a peachy babe here. Sweet tempered and smart."

Doc pressed a kiss on Polly's temple. "Yes, she is. I'm hoping Ginny Mae takes after her."

Peter laughed and slid the baby back into her mother's arms. *Someday, April and me—we'll have a passel of young'uns of our own. I'm biding my time, Lord, but 'twouldn't make me sad if You hurried things along a mite.*

"I made the lotion for you." Polly nodded toward her husband's desk. "There's some for Greta and Kate, too. Peter, I made a salve there for Tempy to use on Artemis's rash. That little baby has the most sensitive skin!"

"Thankee. Aunt Tempy's frettin' like Artemis is her first 'stead of her tenth baby."

"I'll try to get out to the ranch tomorrow or the next day." Polly smiled at April. "I'll help you wash your hair."

"I'd be grateful. Kate's too busy to do it. I'm not sure when Greta will come home. Caleb is moping around without her."

"You've got yore hands full already, Polly. Johnna cain traipse over to holp April. Fact is, Ma and Aunt Eunice are puttin' up tomatoes today. They plan to show up o'er at Chance Ranch to do the same tomorrow."

"But I—"

Peter pressed a finger against April's lips. "Now hush." Despite his desire to do otherwise, he broke contact. "Greta's away, and Kate cain't do it all on her own. With yore hands all burnt, them tomatoes would go to waste. We cain't abide seein' good food squandered. Plenty's the time you stood at the

MacPherson stove in our times of need."

"If you expose those blisters to any heat, they'll worsen," Doc said. "Best thing for you is to use Polly's lotion three times a day."

"Here's a sugar sack for you to carry the things out to the buckboard." Polly smiled as she handed the small cloth bag to Peter. "Tell Eunice to use it to make Elvera a bodice or little skirt."

"Lookie thar. Hit's got yeller kittens all o'er." He chuckled. "It stretches my mind to believe Hezzie's a-gonna teach Elvera the difference 'twixt a kitty and a skunk."

"She was really cute," April said.

"Being cute didn't take off the stink."

"To hear Eunice tell the story," Polly said, "the juice from every last tomato in your garden didn't, either."

"I'm surprised they're canning tomatoes today." Doc grinned. "I didn't think you'd have any left."

"God gave us a bumper crop of 'em." Peter grinned. "Guess it proves how He knows our needs even afore we know 'bout them." He tucked the lotions and salve into the sack. "We'll be headin' out now."

When they reached the buckboard, April set a hand on the front wheel and started to put her foot on a spoke so she could climb up. Peter yanked her back and turned her around. "I'd be pleased to holp you up, miss."

Once they were seated and he'd headed out of town, he gave April an arch look. "You cain't be jumpin' outta the buckboard or scramblin' in like a schoolgirl in pigtails."

Quick as a bunny, she turned her head away.

Peter reached over and pressed against her right cheek, forcing her to face him. "What's got into you?"

"Nothing."

"I got me sisters and girl cousins. One thang I ken: when any of 'em say 'nothin,' it's sommat big. Suppose you level with me."

A mirthless laugh burst out of her. "Something big. That's me."

"You cain't be tellin' me yore afeared I cain't heft you into a buckboard!"

"*Heft*. That says it all." Her face felt hot as embers beneath his fingers, and she lowered her lashes to keep from looking him in the eyes.

"When sommat has a right feel in a man's hand, he says it's got a nice heft. When I wrap my hands 'round yore middle— hope you don't take offense at me speakin' plainly—you fill my hands real good." He nodded. "Yup. You do. Me sayin' *heft*—well, you oughta take that as a compliment."

April pulled away and covered her eyes and forehead with her palm. Fingers and thumb rubbed her temples as she muttered, "You've never had a sweetheart. What am I thinking, listening to your advice? This isn't going to work."

"Hold it thar just a minute."

She gave him a baleful glare.

Aware his plan was in jeopardy, Peter hurriedly said, "This bargain could benefit us both. Mayhap you could fill me in on a gal's view on matters."

"You have sisters."

"And you've got brothers. Fact is, it cain be dreadful embarrassing to share yore innermost fears and failures with 'em."

April nodded.

"I didn't say 'haul,' so suppose you tell me what a gal would rather have a buck say."

"Lift." She gave him a timid, half-smile. "You *lift* a lady into a wagon."

"Okay." He smiled at her. "From now on, April, yore to wait for me to lift you in and out of the wagons. And yore s'posed to smile at me when I do. You got a smile that quickens a man's heart. Why, any buck watchin' is gonna be pea green with envy that I'm the one helping you."

"He's liable to be grateful he's not risking his back."

Peter heaved a loud sigh. "You gotta stop that. Any man who's afeared he cain't *lift* a woman oughtn't be courtin' at all. He should be visitin' Doc to figger out what ails him!"

He drove a little farther, then pulled back on the reins. "Whoa."

"Is something wrong? Why did we stop?"

"On account of it bein' lunchtime." He hopped down, went around to April, and raised his hands toward her.

"I need to get home, Peter."

"Horsefeathers."

"Truly, I do need to get home. I shouldn't have left in the first place."

"You cain tell a feller you ought to be home—that lets him know yore mindful of your obligations. But when you insist and he knows 'tisn't absolutely essential, he's gonna be insulted. Hit's like tellin' him you'd rather be scrapin' yore knuckles on a washboard 'stead of spendin' time with him."

"But we're just pretending."

"Cain't pretend when you don't do it." Peter grinned at her. "Now don't you be challenging what I jist said. You ken full well I meant iff'n you don't practice like yore out courtin' with some fine buck, then you'll like as not miss out on learning sommat important."

To his delight, she stood. Closing his hands around her waist, he ordered, "Now lay your hands atop my shoulders." She complied. He lifted a little, then drew her down. Instead of letting go, he rumbled, "Now don't turn loose of me quick. Wait a bit afore you draw back yore hands."

"How long?"

Forever. "Long 'nuff to look me in the eyes and whisper a sweet little thankee."

"Thank you." She broke contact, then gave him a funny look. "When do you let go?"

Never. "A man is a bit slow to turn loose 'cuz he's taken a shine to a gal. Iff'n a man keeps holt of you too long, you cain twist free or tromp on his toe to make him mind his manners."

"You still haven't let go."

He grinned. When April tried to twist, he held tight. Her eyes widened, then she chewed on her bottom lip. A second later, he chuckled. "Was that a mouse skitterin' 'cross my boot?"

She stepped a little harder, and he let go.

"There. I pretended."

"And you learnt sommat." He pivoted and pulled a blanket from the back of the buckboard.

"Peter!" She looked just as shocked as she sounded. Staring at the blanket, April stammered, "You said we were just pretending. We're not really going to plop down out here in the middle of nowhere and waste time!"

"Lookie how beautiful 'tis here. A field full of posies, a gentle breeze, and 'nuff shade to let you keep your ladylike complexion. A place like this ain't nowhere. 'Tis God's spread. Takin' the opportunity to 'preciate it—that ain't wastin' time." He grabbed the lunch Ma had packed for them and said, "Now you slide yore hand in the crook of my arm."

April balked. "That seems awfully. . .forward."

"Nah. What with women's shoes having them silly heels, and us bein' at a spot where the ground's uneven, hit's common sense for a woman to seek a steadying arm. Now iff'n you grabbed for my hand, that would be forward."

When he winged his elbow toward her, she slid her hand into the crook and sighed. "I don't know if I'll ever remember all of this."

"Don't expect you to, all at once. Practice makes perfect. We'll make shore we get together a bunch."

They spread out the blanket, then sat side by side. Curling his hand around hers, Peter said, "I'm tryin' to be mindful of yore fingers. When first you have picnics with other bucks, don't go lettin' 'em hold yore hand. Me? Well, both of our families practice linkin' hands for grace. Wouldn't seem right, us prayin' without doin' this."

"Even when there are just two of us?"

"Bible says where two or three are gathered, God's in the midst. Two's plenty." He bowed his head. "Dear lovin' Lord, thankee for April and givin' us time together. I ask Yore blessin' on our endeavors and on the food we eat. Be with our kin, where'er they be, amen."

"Amen." After emptying the buckets, April took one of the cloths and spread it across her lap.

"All you Chances—you got elegant table manners. What say you holp me learn some of 'em?"

"I'd be happy to. The first thing you do after prayer is spread a napkin across your lap."

"Why? Food ain't gonna drop 'til after you served up everything."

"It keeps everyone from grabbing."

"Seems easy 'nuff for a woman. Men don't 'zactly have a lap." He chose one thigh and draped the cloth over it. "And I'd thank a woman'd be gratified to see folks pouncin' on her food. Shows they like her cookin'."

April unwrapped a pair of sandwiches and served him one. "Oh, it's your mama's chicken salad! I don't know what she adds to it, but her chicken salad's the best I've ever tasted."

"Says hit's a secret. Johnna had to vow she'd not tell a soul other than her own daughter someday. I 'spect Ma'll share the ingredients with my bride." He waggled his brows. "How bad d'you wanna have that recipe?"

April laughed.

Honey pie, you don't know how serious I am.

Her laughter suddenly died out. "Peter! What did you tell your mother? She has to know something's up, or she wouldn't have made this lunch!"

"I tole her the truth—that yore a special gal and I wouldn't mind passin' more time with you."

"Peter! They're going to think—"

"I don't live my life frettin' o'er what other folks thank. Neither should you. Iff'n yore shore what you do is pleasin' to the Almighty, that's the only measure what counts."

"Yes, but—"

His heart twisted. "April, are you ashamed to have folks believe I've taken a shine to you?"

five

"Don't be ridiculous!" The immediacy of April's response made it clear that embarrassment wasn't the issue. "Peter, if folks think you're courting me, then you can't be free to follow your heart when the right girl comes along."

"You oughtta be more worried 'bout fellers who won't come callin' on you 'cuz I am."

"Have you taken leave of your senses? I've never caught the attention of anyone."

Peter snorted. "So you say. You hang onto yore hat, April Chance. Men always want what they cain't get. Soon as fellers see me 'round you, they'll be kickin' theirselves for not seeing you in a true light. I'm gonna make 'em jealous. Won't be long afore they beat a path to yore door."

"You're not making sense. In one breath, you tell me men won't come calling because we're seen together. In the next breath, you tell me they'll be beating a path out to the ranch."

"That's 'cuz you don't understand the plan yet." He took a big bite of his sandwich.

Looking completely disgruntled, April took a bite of hers.

"Here's how it works. Folks is gonna link yore name and mine. Soon 'nuff, the fellers'll take notice. You'll be yore friendly self to them, but I'll still have you on my arm. With me squirin' you about, they're gonna have to contend with me. Me? I'm gonna gloat aloud 'bout how wonderful them sticky buns are that you make." He lifted his sandwich, and just before taking a good-sized chomp out of it, he tacked on, "Yore gonna make me them sticky buns so I'm not bein' a liar, right?"

"I make them every Wednesday."

"But when you up and bake 'em any other day, yore kin are gonna take notice. Smack their hands away and tell 'em that whole batch is for me. Things like that make an impression. Won't be long afore someone on Chance Ranch goes to town and grumbles."

"I'm beginning to wonder if all of this is a ploy to get me to bake you a batch."

Peter set down his sandwich and looked at her. "Woman, I'm fixin' to give you a lecture, so pay me heed."

Her eyes widened.

"First off, I'm a straightforward kinda man. If all I wanted was yore sticky buns, I'd tromp up and tell you so. Second, I have no patience with a man who stoops to dally with a gal's heart. Most of all, yore worthy of love and respect jist for bein' you. 'Tis the truth. God gave you a special gift."

"Gift?"

"Gal, thank on this: Ever'body cain sing, but some got a special voice. Same is true 'bout cookin'. Most every woman— 'cept for Polly—cain cook. But when you step into a kitchen, what comes out is a masterpiece. I'll be shore to praise yore talent, but don't you e'er make the mistake of thankin' yore only worth is a batch of sommat you pull outta the oven. Someday, like the Bible says, yore young'uns are gonna rise up and call you blessed, and a lucky man will value you far above rubies."

If he hadn't been sitting next to her, the longing in April's eyes would have knocked him to his knees. Peter said softly, "I believe it. Deep in my heart, I do."

"Peter?"

"Yeah?"

"You're an extraordinary man. Truly, you are. Why haven't you gone courting? Plenty of girls would be flattered to receive your attention."

He shook his head. "Not the right time yet. God's got someone special for me, and I'm fine with waitin' 'til He brings her along."

"You're not impatient?"

"At times, but most often not." He picked up what was left of his sandwich. "Shore was nice of you to speak well of me. I'm a simple farm boy, and I'm oddly spoken. My kin—we have all we need, but others prob'ly thank the MacPhersons are dirt poor."

"You're a hard-working man. Strong and handsome. As for your dialect—I find it charmingly expressive. In many ways, it resembles the phrasing of the King James language in our Bible."

"Niver thought of it thataway."

"Well, I have. When it comes to the MacPherson clan— you're all content with what God's given you. You're rich in the things that matter most: love, family, friends, and health. Any woman who can't appreciate that doesn't deserve you."

Peter stared at her. For so long, he'd wondered what she thought about those issues. She didn't have to search at all to come up with any of those fine words. The praise just flowed out of her, and he knew the sentiments were heartfelt. *If only she'd come to feel all of those things specially for me.*

He cleared his throat. "You shore said a mouthful."

"I meant every bit of it."

"Even though I don't tuck my napkin in my lap, first off?"

April laughed and yanked his hand from his mouth just before he licked his fingers. "Don't lick, Peter. Use the napkin! As for table manners—those can be learned in a trice. Character is developed over a lifetime. A woman would be a fool to choose a so-called gentleman with poor moral fiber over a rough man with integrity who's proven his devotion to God and family."

"Yore sweet words are better than dessert."

"I don't know. . . . We have grapes and Aunt Tempy's delicious cheese."

He looked into her lovely blue eyes. "The day couldn't get more perfect."

за

"The day couldn't get any worse." Matt Salter stared at the back of the buggy that carried away a weeping woman. "Her whole world has been destroyed."

"Bootleg moonshine." The San Francisco sheriff shook his head. "Killed her son and blinded her husband."

"Where's it coming from?"

Sheriff Charles S. Laumeister turned to go back inside the building. "Not sure."

"Anybody check orders for copper piping or large orders of sugar?"

Laumeister shot him a grin. "You'll be doing that. I'm putting two of you on special detail. Miller is canvassing south of here. You'll go east."

"Lot of land out there. Bootleggers could have multiple stills in operation."

"I expect they do." The sheriff sat behind his desk and shrugged. "I don't want you nabbing someone who's distilling a jug or two a week."

Matt didn't respond. It would be a waste of breath. Plenty of farmers and ranchers distilled small amounts of spirits for themselves. Rounding them up would be ludicrous.

"I want to put down the major source. There's a big operation out there somewhere. Pose as a man in need of work. You can drift from one area to the next. No one'll suspect a saddle tramp of being a lawman."

A wry smile tugged at the corner of Matt's mouth. "I was a saddle tramp before I became a deputy."

"Precisely why this case is suited to you."

"Folks are closed-mouthed. Finagling the necessary information means I'll have to earn their trust. That takes time."

Laumeister nodded. "I want a thorough job. Get to the heart of the operation. Keep in contact—once a week's fine."

"That's the fastest way to blow my cover. Places where there's a still, most of the locals know about it. Too risky for me to check in regularly."

"Do your best."

"That goes without saying. I'll have to give up my room at the boardinghouse."

"No loss. I've tasted Jenny's cooking. Burned baked beans'll be a treat by comparison. You can stow a trunk in the storage room here. Get going."

Matt strode out of the office, down the street, and into the boarding house. A wool blanket, one Sunday-go-to-meeting white shirt and string tie, a passably good pair of britches the color of charcoal, a pair of just-this-side-of-disreputable work shirts, and his Levis. . .that's about all a rover would have aside from his hat and saddle.

Matt changed into the red shirt and denims. A rodeo buckle he'd won a few years back gave the finishing touch. Rolling up the remainder, he realized he'd need a bandana. *Good. It gives me an excuse to mosey into a mercantile and pick up on gossip.* He picked up the roll and opened his door.

"Mr. Salter, whatever are you doing?" Miss Jenny asked from the hallway.

He turned around and looked at the homely old spinster. Bless her, she worked hard to earn an honest living. She couldn't cook worth two hoots, yet she tried her best. In the year and a half that he'd lived here, Matt had grown to respect her. He even paid for both room and board though he rarely ate any lunch or supper there. That way, she still had a tiny bit more in her pocket.

"Miss Jenny, you run a fine place. The bed's comfortable, and you wash sheets every week. I'm going to miss that, but—"

"You're leaving." Her lower lip trembled. "It's the cowboy in you, isn't it? You long to sleep out under the stars."

"It's been a long while since I have."

"You're a fine young man. I'll be praying for you. Would it be too forward of me to ask you to drop me a note every now and then? Just to make sure you haven't gotten murdered in your sleep by some nefarious bandit?"

She'd been reading too many dime novels. Then again, aside from working and studying her Bible, what did Miss Jenny have to fill her hours? Matt nodded. "I'll be sure to write you a line or two."

"I do appreciate that. I'll bake a going-away cake for you. We'll have it after supper tonight."

"Miss Jenny, that's as kind as can be, but I'm going to leave right after I pack the rest of my things." He dug in his pocket and pulled out a golden eagle. "This is for you."

"Oh, no. I couldn't! Mr. Salter, that's ten dollars!"

"It might take you awhile to get a new boarder in. Since I didn't give you notice, it only seems fair."

She shook her head. "I can't take that. You're already paid clear through the end of next month. Truthfully, I ought to give you a refund."

"Let's not spoil our last few minutes together quibbling." He pressed the coin into her hand.

"God bless you, Mr. Salter."

"He does. May He bless you as well."

A scant hour later, Matt swung up into the saddle and headed east. At sunset, he reached the outskirts of a sleepy little town and spent the night outside. Hot as it was, he didn't need a fire—but his clothes lacked the smell of wood smoke and needed a touch of authentic ground-in grime. He'd bought a box supper right before leaving San Francisco. After eating the meal, he used the pasteboard box as tinder to start a fire.

By the time dawn arrived, he glanced down at his rumpled shirt and grinned. Roughing it for one night resulted in just the right disguise.

❧

"Mornin'." He doffed his hat toward the old lady and gent at the counter of the mercantile of the nearby town.

"Never seen you before," the old man said.

"I'm just passing through. Lost my bandana."

The woman toddled out and beckoned him. "I have a whole stack of them over here."

Matt sauntered over and thumbed through the stack. "Nice ones. Sorta fancy." He gave her a crooked smile. "Last one I had was part of a sugar sack. Yellow. I was partial to that."

The old woman chortled softly. "You'll not find a yellow sugar sack on any shelf for miles around."

"Why?"

"Because the MacPhersons in Reliable buy all their sugar in yellow sacks."

"Is that a fact?"

The old woman's head bobbed.

He pretended to thumb through the rest of the stack and mused in a laconic voice, "Seems like a lot of sugar."

"Been like that for years. Those are first-rate bandanas. No skimping on the size. Edges done by machine with small stitches that won't give out under hard use."

"Yup." After patting the stack, he took the uppermost. "This'll do." He headed for the counter. As he was paying, his stomach growled.

"The diner's open across the street," the old man said.

"Now, Daddy," the old woman chided, "sending this young man over there's almost a crime." She waddled closer and clucked her tongue. "New folks from back East just bought it. Charging half again what the old prices were and serving smaller portions."

"Mama, it's their business. They can set whatever price they want."

"They won't stay in business long that way. When the diner doesn't draw folks to stop in, we won't have as many customers, either."

"We'll get more customers. Folks are bound to buy more groceries when they get a gander at the prices over yonder."

Matt gave the couple a curt nod, picked up the bandana, and walked out. Bickering irritated him. Instead of going to the diner, he rode toward the next town. Learning that the MacPhersons of Reliable used considerable quantities of sugar on a regular basis led him in that direction.

By midday, Matt reckoned even Miss Jenny's cooking would taste pretty good. He hitched his horse to the post outside of Joe's Eats. A burly man in a stained apron waved his arm toward the room. "Have a seat. Coffee?"

Matt nodded. He'd discovered if he let the other person start talking, they were more likely to give information as he subtly steered the conversation.

Thump. A mug hit the table. "I've got catfish, ham sandwiches, and ribs. Whaddya want?"

"How fresh is the catfish?"

"Billy there," the aproned man jabbed his thumb to the left, "caught a mess of 'em this morning. I add cayenne pepper to the cornmeal to give 'em a kick, so if you've got a sissy-mouth, choose something else."

"I'll take catfish."

A slow smile lit the cook's face. "Double the cayenne?"

"Triple."

Billy leaned way back in his chair. "You don't know what you're asking for."

"The hotter, the better." Matt lifted the coffee mug and took a long, loud slurp. After enduring Miss Jenny's weak-as-dishwater coffee each morning, this stuff tasted strong. He nodded approvingly. "Cup of this could wake a dead man."

Chuckling as he headed toward the kitchen, the cook asked, "Staying around very long?"

"Don't know."

The man across from Billy shoved the last of a biscuit into his mouth and spoke around the food. "Itchy feet?"

"Show me a cowboy who doesn't have itchy feet," Billy shot back.

"Or a powerful thirst," the first man said.

Matt took another gulp, then set down the mug and twisted it slowly from side to side. "There's strong coffee; then there's strong whiskey."

Billy snorted. "Not around here. The Tankard waters down all of the liquor."

"Now that," Matt paused meaningfully, "is a crime." He'd spoken the truth. It was criminal to represent goods to a customer and purposefully give him less than he paid for. Nonetheless, Matt knew full well these men would take the comment in another light.

"A sorry circumstance," Bill agreed.

"Then the emporium—"

Billy scoffed. "The old coot at the mercantile won't sell spirits. Says it's the devil's brew. If a man here wants decent whiskey, he goes off to the city and brings himself back a supply."

"And he's got to reckon with his neighbors if he doesn't take an order from them." The other man smacked his hand on the table and bellowed, "More coffee!"

"Come get the pot yourself," the cook hollered.

"Some way to treat a paying customer," the man muttered as he rose.

Billy shoveled a heaping forkful of peas in, chewed all of twice, then swallowed. "Pennington's usually looking for another hand. Can't keep 'em long. Won't abide a man who takes a nip now and then. One of those holier-than-thou sorts. Everyone on his spread has to go to church. He's got no call, telling men what to do during the time they call their own."

"Can't keep the help for long, huh?"

"Nope. And his daughters are uglier than a mud-stuck fence." Billy shuddered. "Buck-toothed and horse-faced. A feller might turn a blind eye to that if he knew when the old man passed on, he'd get the ranch."

"But he won't?"

"He brought in a nephew last year. Greenhorn from back East."

Matt grimaced.

"I swear," Billy said, "there's more air between that Easterner's ears than there is under the crown of his ten-gallon hat."

The other man returned with the coffee pot. "Best you fill that cup of yours with milk, mister. Much cayenne as Sam put on your catfish, your mouth is gonna beg for mercy."

"I'll handle it." Matt knew the game. These men were taking his measure. It wouldn't hurt if he got a few folks talking about him. . .as long as it cast him in light of a tough, ready-to-work wrangler. He'd mentioned his experience. There was no way for these men to check it out, but by downing the punishingly hot catfish, he'd prove himself.

He lifted his mug and accepted the refill with a nod. "So

Pennington is out. I'm looking for something short-term, but if I take a nip of who-hit-John, I don't want the job to be over. I leave on my terms, not theirs."

The cook came out with a plate. He placed it in front of Matt, then pulled out the chair directly across from him and took a seat. "Give 'er a taste."

"Don't mind if I do." He speared a chunk, popped it into his mouth, chomped a few times, and swallowed. "Now that's catfish!" He took another bite.

"Like it?" The cook gave him a sly look.

"It'll do. Don't mean to insult you, but do you have any Tabasco?"

As Matt doused the fish with Tabasco, he asked, "Any other spreads looking for help?"

"Could be the Berlews would hire you on. That kid's a skinflint, though. More than one cowboy's walked away with less in his pocket than Berlew promised."

"Is that a fact?" Matt mumbled that comment without intending it as a question. It would merely serve to keep the conversation going.

"He's got prime breeding stock and plenty of pasture. His granddaddy kicked the bucket and left the place to him. Won't come as no surprise if he runs it into the ground by the time he's thirty."

Matt washed down the last bite of fish with a long swallow of coffee. "Well, sounds like I'd better hit the road if I wanna find me work. Places hereabouts don't sound much to my liking."

The cook stared at Matt's empty plate with nothing short of admiration. "Somebody's gotta want a man like you."

Billy perked up. "Hey—d'ya only run cows, or will you work horses?"

"I'm not choosy."

"Next town east of here is Reliable. Chance Ranch puts out the best saddle horses you'll ever see."

The cook stood and wiped his hands down the front of his apron. "They hardly ever hire help."

Billy rapped his knuckles on the table. "Might be that they would. A bunch of the Chance men left for a while. Handful of young'uns are running the place."

Men leaving for a spell might mean they were up to something. If their horse ranch was so successful, few things would promise profits great enough to entice them away. Moonshining was lucrative. The facts added up to paint a suspicious picture. The MacPhersons who bought all that sugar were from Reliable, too. Either family or both could be involved. Matt mused, "Chance Ranch, huh?"

six

Shoving back several damp curls that had escaped her precarious bun, Kate wilted onto a bench in the yard. "I'm beat."

April laughed. "Is that your way of saying you'd rather watch the kids the next time?"

"I'm going to write a letter to the Ball Mason company and ask them to make thirty-gallon jars." Kate grinned at her. "It would be a whole lot easier to can kids and watch vegetables."

"You have a point," April said. "I'm sorry I couldn't help."

Shaking her head, Kate turned toward her and said, "You're not the one who ought to apologize. I should. You've always helped with the canning. Most years, I either watched the kids or managed to be busy with some other project."

Peter sauntered up. "Well? Get a lot done?"

"I'm not sure," Kate confessed. "For all the work we did in the kitchen, it doesn't seem like all that much when I look at the results. How can it take that much work to fill up those quart jars?"

"It takes four jars to feed everyone just one supper."

"April," Kate moaned, "did you have to say that?"

Giving her a sweet smile, April said, "Well, it would only take two right now with half of the family gone."

Peter chuckled as he stepped to April's side and casually poked in a few of her hairpins as if they needed attention—even though they didn't. "But yore using fresh-picked truck right now. See how much work yore saving?"

Laughter bubbled out of Kate. "Only you would point that out. Are you staying for supper?"

52

"Will it be more work for you?"

Kate pretended to glower at him. "You know you're always welcome here. There's always plenty of food, too."

A stranger rounded the edge of one of the cabins. He yanked off his hat, revealing sable hair and deeply tanned features. A couple of days' worth of whiskers sandpapered his jaw. "Ladies, sir." He nodded, then rode his palomino a little closer before dismounting.

"Lose your way?" Peter asked as he stepped in front of Kate and April. Kate wanted to push him out of the way. Then again, she used the shield he created to reach up to swiftly tuck hairpins back into place and lift the corner of her apron to blot her face.

"Hope not. Sign at the entrance said CHANCE RANCH. I'm looking for work. I'm Matt Salter."

Peter stepped forward and shook hands. "Peter MacPherson. I'm the neighbor to the east."

Kate leaned to the side to see Mr. Salter's face. His smile robbed him of the disreputable look days in the saddle lent.

"MacPherson," Mr. Salter repeated. "You must belong to that buckboard that just went by me on the road."

Peter chuckled. "Were they all still singing at the top of their lungs?"

"Seemed like they were enjoying themselves." Mr. Salter's brown eyes sparkled as he tacked on, "Only time I ever saw that much yellow in one place was standing in front of the corncrib right after a husking."

Popping to her feet, Kate added, "I'd be willing to bet there were more children in the buckboard than there were ears of corn in the crib."

"Ma'am." Mr. Salter gave her a mannerly nod as he said, "I'd be hard pressed to disagree."

"It's *miss*," Kate said.

Peter cleared his throat loudly to drown out her words. "The Chance men'll be by directly. You'll need to talk with them."

"Thanks. Mind if I water my horse?"

"Please do." Kate couldn't get out another word before Peter took hold of her arm and pulled her around.

"Ladies, 'tisn't fittin' to leave Mr. Salter out here on his lonesome. I'll keep him company whilst you tend to the supper." Peter pulled April to her feet and prodded them toward the kitchen.

Kate didn't want to go back into the kitchen. She'd been there all day, canning beans, corn, peas, and tomatoes. Even with the doors open so the air would blow through the screens, the place still felt hot as could be.

April hooked her arm through Kate's. "We need to plan tomorrow's menu, anyway."

As soon as they got into the cabin, Kate pulled away from her cousin. "What was that all about? Any time a wrangler comes through, the least we do is invite him to stay to supper."

"Quiet down," April hissed. "We normally have five more men, five more women, and a half-dozen kids here, too. Peter's being cautious, and it's for our welfare."

"That man has honest eyes. Steady, deep brown, never-let-you-down eyes. He's taken good care of his mount, too. Uncle Bryce swears you can tell a lot about a man by how he cares for his horse."

"When the boys come in, they can decide whether he's staying for supper."

"I vote that he stays—for supper, and for a job."

"You're not old enough to vote," April reminded her. "You won't be twenty-one for almost a year yet."

Kate winced. The family's rule stood strong. Any member was given a vote on matters as soon as they reached their twenty-first birthday. "Caleb, Tobias, and you are the only ones who have votes. Well, Greta, too, but she's not here. So you have to vote in favor of him, April."

"Why are you taking on so?"

"We could use the help," Kate muttered. She turned toward the stove and grabbed a potholder. By keeping her back to April, she might manage to hide her feelings.

"Just yesterday, you were saying how well we've done on our own."

Kate opened the oven door and moved the huge roasters full of casserole around. They didn't necessarily require that action, but it kept her busy. "We have done well, but it would be good to hire a little help so we could accomplish a few extra projects before everyone gets home."

"We're expecting the family to get home any day now."

"See? That proves that we'd better grab this opportunity." Kate shut the oven door and turned around. "There's no telling when another man will be by."

April gave her a knowing grin. "I have a funny feeling there's something about this particular man that has you angling for him to stay."

"He's young and healthy, and he has fine manners." Kate stared at her cousin. "Not that you'd notice. You and Peter are so besotted with one another, it could rain pie tins and neither of you would notice."

Cheeks turning scarlet, April squeaked, "Kate!"

"Don't bother to deny it. Peter's hovering over you. He even fussed with your hairpins out there when they didn't need any attention at all." April looked ready to say something, so Kate plowed ahead, "Just now, Peter protected you from that stranger—even though no danger existed."

"Peter protected both of us. And you can't say for certain that Mr. Ummm. . ."

"Salter," Kate provided.

"Yes. Well, you can't vouch for Mr. Salter. Plenty of women have been beguiled and deceived by charming men."

"He was charming, wasn't he?" Kate stirred the peas.

"Add a pinch of sugar to that water. The peas always taste better if you do."

"So that's your secret!" Kate meant to put in a dab. Almost half a cup plopped into the boiling pot. "Oh, no!"

April hopped up and grabbed the colander. "Dump them in this right away!" She placed it in the sink as Kate grabbed hot pan holders.

"Do you know how many peas I shelled to get this pot?"

"I have a pretty fair notion," April said wryly. "Now rinse them off. We'll cover them with water we dip out of the reservoir. It'll be hot enough to keep them warm 'til we slather them with butter."

As she rinsed off the peas then jumbled them back into the pot, Kate said, "You never slather peas with butter. You barely even dot them with it."

"Exactly." April winked. "This is a new recipe. We'll see how the men like it."

Kate dipped hot water from the stove reservoir and quickly covered the peas. "I never did get around to making dessert."

"Pull out two cake pans." April walked over to the far side of the room. April often measured out an extra set of the dry ingredients for a recipe she was making. She stored that set away in jars on the bottom shelf of the copper-punch-fronted pie safe.

"Oh, bless you!" Kate finished covering the peas with water, then grabbed for the cake pans.

April drew four, one-quart jars from the bottom shelf. Cradling them in her arms, she headed toward the table.

"We need melted butter. While you do that, I'll measure out the vinegar, vanilla, and water."

"Ohhh," Kate breathed. "Crazy cake?"

Bobbing her head, April said, "I think I can manage to mix one while you do the other. You can take the casseroles out of the oven and pop in the cakes. By the time supper's over, the cakes will be done."

"As I recall, Peter loves your crazy cake," Kate said.

April didn't meet her eyes. She urged, "Hurry up and get to work. You can't go back out there looking like we stirred your hair with an egg beater."

❧

"You're welcome to stay to supper." Caleb Chance smacked his leather work gloves against the side of his jeans, making dust fly.

Matt nodded. "Appreciate the invite. I'm hungry enough to eat the legs off a lizard."

"As for a job," Caleb warned, "I'll get back to you on that later this evening."

"Fair enough." A grin stretched across Matt's face. "Maybe better than fair. Decent food's been known to put men into a good frame of mind."

The blond gal with the cute freckles stepped onto the porch of a cabin. "Supper's ready. Tanner, go wash up."

"Awww, Kate—"

"Just 'cuz Mama's not here, that doesn't give you call to come to the table gritty as the path you rode today. You P's, come fetch the dishes. C's, you can carry out the food."

"P's and C's?" Matt looked to Caleb for an explanation.

"Brothers all have names starting with the same letter."

"Tanner is Kate's brother?"

"Yup. Girls got named whatever the mother fancied. April's my sis."

Matt murmured, "If MacPherson has his way, it won't be

long before she's his wife."

Caleb's features darkened as he snarled, "They're cousins."

"My mistake." The sinking feeling that he'd ruined any opportunity to hire on assailed Matt. He shrugged. "Guess that's why I haven't gotten hitched. Never could figure out a woman."

In scant minutes, food and dishes appeared on the table. The women sat at the end of one of the two abutted tables. Matt made it a point to head toward the extreme other end.

"You jist lay yore hand atop mine," Peter told April. "That-away, I won't hurt yore burns none." When April complied, Peter's smile could put the moon out of business.

Cousins or not, that man's chasing that woman.

To Matt's astonishment, everyone linked hands. "I'll ask the blessing," one of the men offered. Matt bowed his head.

As prayers went, it was short and to the point. After the "amen," men yanked the napkins from the table, draped them in their laps, and grabbed for the nearest dish.

Not an hour ago, red-headed Peter MacPherson could have made a prosecuting attorney run for cover with all the questions he'd posed. Once the Chance men came from all parts of the property for supper, they'd been just as nosey. These men must not have heard of the Code of the West where a man's past was nobody's business but his own.

The way the Chances acted so guarded made Matt's suspicions rise. Added to that, the fact that a MacPherson happened to be here made the association between his two prime suspects all that more important. Matt refused to allow a brief prayer to fool him. The Chance men all had deep brown hair and blue eyes, but their features were dissimilar enough for Matt to tell them apart. He'd always been good with names—a skill that stood him in good stead since he'd met all eight of them in a matter of minutes.

Packard swiped the saltshaker from Tanner. "That foal looking any better?"

"Yup." Tanner shoveled in a huge bite and spoke around the food, "He's feelin' good enough to be ornery."

"Ohhh, man. Buttered sweet peas." The words escaped Matt's mouth. Feeling a little sheepish, he tacked on, "I haven't had these since I left home."

"Kate made them," April said. "They're a new recipe."

"Not bad, sis," one of the men said.

Kate beamed. The woman's whole face lit up when she smiled. She said, "April and I have crazy cake in the oven for dessert."

"I volunteer to go pull it outta the oven," Peter said.

Bellows of laughter met that comment. When they died down a little, Caleb said, "That's like having the fox mind the chicken coop."

"Cain't blame a feller for tryin'. Only thang better'n April's crazy cake is her sticky buns."

April blushed. "As soon as my hands are better, I'll bake a batch of them especially for you."

Every man around the table suddenly froze. Forks hung midair. Conversation halted mid-sentence. Matt pretended not to be entertained by the variety of expressions—some eyes widened in surprise, while others narrowed with anger.

seven

"I thank yore brothers and cousins are het up o'er me claiming a batch all to myself."

"And who'd blame them?" Kate laughed. "You know Chances always share."

"Kate," Caleb gritted, "you stay outta this. Peter"—he jerked his thumb over his shoulder—"behind the stable."

"What's gotten into you, Caleb?" April looked down the table at her brother.

"Yore big brother thanks yore too young to court." Peter's voice held an entertained lilt.

"He started courting Greta when he was younger than I am."

Caleb stood. The muscles in his jaw twitched. "Behind the stable. Now."

Peter rose. "Kate, would you please make shore the cake don't burn? 'Twould be a dreadful pity iff'n this little mis-understandin' ruint dessert."

"Don't bother, Kate," Caleb said. "Peter won't be staying for dessert."

"Caleb, you sit right back down." Kate scooted off the end of the bench. "You're the eldest here, and April's your little sister. But you need to cool off."

"Kate—" Caleb snapped out her name.

"Hold it right there." Matt stood. "Whatever's wrong here can still be reckoned out peacefully, but nobody's going to talk to a woman in that tone of voice when I'm around."

"Mister, sit down, shut your mouth, and finish your meal."

Caleb never turned his glower off Peter as he added, "You'll be leaving as soon as you're done."

"That does it, Caleb." Kate threw her napkin on the table. "We've all put up with you being cranky since Greta's at her sister's, but you're downright impossible anymore."

"She's right," one of the men muttered.

"I'm getting the cake out of the oven. When I come back out here, every last one of you had better be sitting here with a smile on his face, or I'm going to do the laundry all by myself again."

Kate left. Peter stared at Caleb. "Ain't gonna be no skin offa my nose if Kate don't rinse the lye outta the skivvies. None of my clothes hang on your clothesline."

"And they never will." Caleb's voice rivaled a thunderclap. "I'll put up with itchy clothes before I let you court my sister."

"I s'pose you cain object all you want, but it'd be mighty nice iff'n you had a decent reason."

"You're cousins!" one of the men shouted.

Peter shook his head. "Two thangs. First off, I'm not deaf. Second, and more importantly, April ain't my cousin."

"Of course, she's your cousin."

"Nope. Polly is a cousin to Tempy's children." Peter grinned as he drawled, "The rest of us ain't related at all."

April laughed. "When we said the Chances share, I guess we took it too far. We claimed aunts and uncles and cousins who actually aren't ours at all."

"Iff'n you still wanna meet me out back 'hind the stable, I'll be happy to oblige." Peter's brows rose. "Haven't e'er had a set-to so's I could whup you, Caleb, but April's more than worth a coupla skinned knuckles."

"He's right," one of the men marveled.

"Right about me whuppin' Caleb, or that April's the finest woman 'round these here parts?"

"We're not cousins," Caleb said slowly. He stepped over the bench, took three quick strides, and smacked Peter on the back. *"Hoo-ooo-ey!"*

Peter returned the hefty slap. "I could still take you on, level you out, and eat the whole cake afore you came to."

While the Chance men all palavered, Matt left the table and headed for his horse. He'd blown his opportunity to hire on here and keep watch on his prime suspects—but he'd find a way to continue surveillance. *I couldn't live with myself if I let a man treat a woman that way.*

"Hey!" A young man hustled over. "You're not going."

"Looks that way."

"You'll have to forgive Caleb. Between his wife being gone and him feeling protective of his sister, he overreacted. Me? I appreciated you sticking up for my sis. If I hadn't been so shocked about Peter and April, I would have pounded Caleb into the ground for snapping at Kate myself."

"Tobias!" Kate yelled from the porch of the kitchen cabin. "You can't send Mr. Salter away until we vote."

"Think hard before you speak," April called to Tobias. "Two crazy cakes hang in the balance."

Tobias rested his hands on his hips. "Caleb, Greta's not here. There's no telling what her opinion on this would be, so that leaves us down to three votes. April and I—we vote this man's staying on as a hired hand. Say what you will, but you're outvoted."

Caleb's chin rose a notch. "He's opinionated."

"Show me a man around here who isn't." Kate stayed on the porch and wiped her hands on the hem of her apron.

"He stuck his nose in where it didn't belong."

"Only to protect my sister." Tobias glared. "I would have called you out a heartbeat later if he hadn't spoken up. There's no excuse for being rude to a lady."

Caleb cleared his throat. "Kate, you have my apology. Peter, you do, too—though I think you were underhanded to sneak up on my sister without asking permission to court her. As for Salter, Tobias, you're wrong. I'm not outvoted. The vote is unanimous: he stays for now."

"Well, what do you think of that?" Kate called.

Tobias slugged Matt in the arm. "Guess it's time we ate dessert. It's crazy cake!"

Matt shook his head. "The cake's not the only thing crazy around here."

★

April closed her eyes and felt Peter gently glide a comb through her just-washed tresses. "Johnna was nice to come help again today."

"Sis reckoned Kate might need holp wringin' out the bedding. Ain't easy to do on yore lonesome."

Opening her eyes, April looked over at Kate and Johnna as they hung another sheet on the clothesline. "I feel so silly. I'm sure I could help out—"

"Hold it right there. Doc said you've gotta keep yore hands clean and dry for a week."

A buggy pulled into the yard, swirling dust all over the place and covering the freshly washed and hung laundry with a coat of grime. "Hello!" Merry laughter filled the air. "I can see I don't need to ask if anyone's home."

"Hi, Lucinda." April forced a smile. She ought to be hospitable, but it wasn't easy. Lucinda's thoughtlessness just made a lot more work for Kate and Johnna. Then, too, at the moment April knew full well she looked like a drowned rat. Lucinda's peach-colored silk dress spread about her on the buggy seat, giving her the appearance of a much-cherished china doll.

Lucinda daintily lifted a gloved hand to her mouth and

gave April a wide-eyed look. "Why, I just cannot fathom what your mama would say if she saw you out here with your hair down, April."

"Her mama would stand here and comb it for her," Peter said as he continued to tease out a stubborn tangle. "Sun dries it right quick."

"My hands are burned," April explained.

"You poor thing. I've never suffered so." Lucinda's dimples deepened as she smiled. "Daddy insists Mama and I. . ." She drew in a dramatic breath. "He says a lady—well, never you mind." She surveyed the yard. "Isn't Tobias here?"

Kate dried her hands on her apron. "My brother is out working."

"Will he be back for luncheon?"

"Doubt it." Peter drew the comb through April's hair again. "Kate sent the boys out with sandwiches."

"Come on down from yore buggy," Johnna invited. "Plenty wants doin'."

"Like rinsing, wringing out, and rehanging the sheets," Kate tacked on.

"That's a fact." Johnna rubbed her cheekbone with the back of her wrist. "Another pair of hands would holp."

As if he sensed April's impulse to rise, Peter's hand curled around her shoulder. Carefully leashed strength held her in place.

Lucinda cast a look toward the clothesline and shrugged as if it were of no concern. "I can't stay. I just can't."

"Then why," Johnna asked, "did you ask if Tobias'd be home for lunch?"

Lucinda ignored the question and held a slip of paper aloft. "I only stopped by on my way home because a telegram came for you."

"Thanks for bringing it by." Kate reached for the message.

"Anything to help a neighbor." Lucinda handed over the telegram. "Oh, and please tell Tobias I'll be expecting him for Sunday supper."

"We've already arranged a picnic with the MacPhersons," Kate said.

"You all go right on ahead. There are so many of you, I'm sure Tobias won't be missed." Lucinda gave them a jaunty wave. "Bye-bye."

"Who's the telegraph from?" Johnna looked over Kate's shoulder.

"Uncle Gideon."

"Daddy!" April popped up. Peter's arm went about her waist.

"He says Yosemite's beautiful. The boys are having a great time. They're traveling slower than planned, and we can expect them to get back home late next week."

"Do you think Aunt Lovejoy's having trouble? Her back—"

"Don't go borrowin' worries," Peter said. "Lovejoy has trouble with her back, but with all the beautiful views, she's probably too busy gawkin' to pay much mind to those twinges."

Kate beamed. "We have a whole week to get extra things done. It's a good thing we hired Mr. Salter."

Johnna elbowed her. "Best we get back to work. No use in gettin' moon-eyed o'er a saddle tramp. Most don't stay more'n a month or so."

Watching the girls go back toward the laundry, April let out a sigh.

"Don't you fret yoreself none 'bout not helping with the wash."

"I'm not," she said glumly.

He drew the comb through her hair once again. "Lucinda has an air about her. 'Tisn't you, April. She prob'ly don't even know she comes 'cross as bein' biggety. Don't let her bother you."

"She doesn't. Her parents dote on her so much, I figure she expects everyone else is supposed to treat her with the same indulgence."

"See? You went and done it again. Plenty of folks would get gossipy and make catty comments. You practically bend o'er backwards to be nice." He set aside the comb and slid his fingers through her hair a time or two before dividing it into three segments.

"You know how to braid?" April turned her head a little to the side to look up at him.

"Nope. But I seen my sisters and cousins and ma plait hair day in and day out. Cain't be all that hard."

Minutes later, April tried not to laugh. Peter had twisted, knotted, and undone a variety of crazy attempts. "Peter, take the left section and put it over the middle one. Then take the right section and put it over the middle. Left, right, left, right. . ."

"So the middle ends up havin' a turn at bein' a side. Ain't that the beatenist?"

From the rhythmic way her hair swished, April could tell he'd achieved the technique. She started to relax a little.

"So iff'n the wash and Lucinda aren't nettlin' you, what is it?"

April tensed. She'd hoped they'd left that sore subject alone. "I think you have the plait long enough. Here's a ribbon to tie at the bottom."

He tied the thin lavender grosgrain ribbon near the end of her waist-length plait, then tickled her cheek with the edge of her braid. "You cain tell me, little April. I'm yore friend, and I wanna share yore woes as well as yore joys."

"I'm drowning in self-pity," April confessed sheepishly. "Lucinda and Tobias are courting. Johnna has Trevor. Last night, that new hand took up Kate's defense. This morning at breakfast, I caught them trading glances. I'm older than Kate, and I truly hoped maybe this summer when Daddy and all of my uncles were gone, one of the local boys would get up some nerve and come calling."

"I cain't say that yore wrong on most of what you said. Then again, any man who's ascairt of yore pa and uncles ain't man enough to come courtin'. Besides, is there anybody 'round these parts who you'd like to marry up with?"

"No," she admitted. After sucking in a quick breath, April added, "But it wouldn't hurt to at least have one man want to take a stroll with me."

"I'm that one." Peter stepped over the bench and straddled it. "You and me—we've been havin' ourselves a nice time, haven't we?"

She nodded.

"Far as I cain see, things is goin' jist as we planned. Betcha most of the folks at church will already have our names linked after last night. 'Stead of you a-sittin' in the Chance pew, yore gonna come sit by my side." He nodded. "Yup. That's where you b'long."

April smiled up at him. "You're such a dear friend, Peter. Truly, you are. I wasn't kidding last night when I promised you a batch of sticky buns. Once my burns have healed, it's the first thing I'll make."

He grinned. "A man couldn't ask much more than that."

"Hey, you two lovebirds!" Johnna walked up. "I do declare, I called you both twice. Yore so set on one another, you didn't hear a word I said!"

"So whaddya want, sis?" Peter didn't jump up or sound in the least flustered at being called lovebirds.

"Didn't seem right, Lucinda expectin' Tobias to turn his back on family plans. She trotted off ere we could say so. Kate and me—we reckon what's easiest is to send word back to the Youngbloods and tell 'em to meet us for Sunday picnic like we already had planned. Lucinda niver has managed to come to one."

"It seems passing strange she hasn't, what with us doin' our clan picnic so often." Peter tucked a small strand of April's hair behind her ear. "Don't you agree, honey pie?"

April nodded. She couldn't quite summon her voice. When she shoved her hair back or one of the Chance women helped with her hair, it didn't feel this way. Peter had taken to tucking in her hairpins, spiraling wayward tresses around his big, rough fingers, and giving her the shivers.

"Tell ya what. Me and April—we'll jaunt right on o'er to the Youngbloods and give 'em the invite. The mister and the missus, too."

"I reckoned you'd volunteer for that." Johnna laughed and shook her forefinger at them. "But you know the rules, Peter."

He gave his sister an affronted look. "Course I do."

"What rules?" April rose as Peter gently cupped her elbow.

He cleared his throat and turned a tad ruddy.

"Us MacPhersons got rules 'bout courtin'," Johnna said. "Hand-holdin's where it ends. No kisses 'til the buck asks for the gal's hand in marriage."

Heat rushed clear up to her hairline. April rasped, "We haven't kissed."

Peter looked her straight in the eyes and murmured, "Not yet."

"Soon, I'd warrant, from the way the both of you are actin'." Johnna sashayed off.

April couldn't look away from Peter and whispered, "I feel like a liar."

"You got no reason to. None atall. There ain't nothin' a-wrong with you and me passin' time together. What other folks make of it. . ." He shrugged and stepped over the bench. "I reckon I oughtta take it as a compliment that they suspect yore acceptin' my suit."

As he said those last words, he cupped April's waist and lifted her to the other side. "Peter!" she squealed.

Kate and Johnna's laughter filled the air.

Peter's smile broadened. "Unh-huh. I'm downright proud to squire you."

eight

"There's an elaborate rig." Matt straightened up and squinted toward the north.

"Yeah," Tanner scoffed. "Belongs to the Youngbloods. Looks like Lucinda took a mind to come pester Tobias."

"You could tell who was in the buggy?"

"Wasn't a matter of seeing. It's a matter of knowing. The Youngbloods are the only ones around these parts with such a fancy rig. Her pa favors his Tennessee Walker, and her ma sends servants to town."

"Mrs. Youngblood doesn't pay calls along with her daughter?"

Tanner shook his head. "On occasion, she invites someone over for tea. That's about it. Lucinda goes to town whenever she gets a notion to. That, and coming here to see Tobias. Otherwise, she doesn't gad about."

Matt shrugged. "No matter where I go, folks are always set on living life on their own terms. Guess it doesn't matter much, as long as they've got a roof, clothes, and food."

Tanner yanked the barbed wire taut. "To my way of thinking, they're missing out if that's all they have."

Matt hammered a staple over the wire and into the fencepost.

"Love of God and family—those are what truly make life worth living." Tanner looked up from the wire. "Man is more than flesh. His heart and soul have needs just as keen as his body."

"Far as I can tell, you've got yourself quite a family."

Tanner chuckled. "This is only a fraction of us Chances. Five sets of adults and six youngsters will be home any day now."

"Five? I only counted three sets of siblings. The C's, the P's, and the T's."

"Yup. Dan and Lovejoy have Polly—but she's the doctor's wife. They live in town. Bryce and Daisy—well, they had Jamie, but he passed on. Cute little guy. One of these years when I have a son of my own, I'm going to name him Jamie. Polly did something similar. Ginny Mae was her sister. Ginny and Jamie died at the same time—diphtheria. Polly's baby girl is named Ginny Mae, and it sorta soothed away the lingering sorrow."

"You just said you're a believer. Don't you think they're in heaven?"

"Absolutely." Tanner swatted at a bothersome fly. "In the depths of grief, that was our comfort. You talk like a man who's skeptical about the Lord."

It might actually help him make connections if he agreed, but Matt refused to. He'd never deny the Lord. He knocked on his chest. "Asked Christ into my heart when I was a schoolboy. Never once regretted it."

A big grin creased Tanner's sunburned face. "So you're a brother."

Matt chuckled. "You Chances really do claim a lot of family."

"You bet. I expect you'll wanna come to church."

Matt nodded and pulled out another staple. "Thanks for the invite."

As they continued to reinforce the stretches where the fence needed help, Matt fought with himself. He wanted to attend worship for all of the right reasons. At the back of his mind, though, he also cataloged how attending church could help his mission.

Almighty Father, You know my heart. My intent is to praise and worship You. Help me keep my priorities straight. I mean You no insult.

"You'll meet most of the folks from Reliable at church. Nearly everyone attends."

"You mean there are more people in this little town than all of the Chances and the MacPhersons?"

Tanned nodded. "You know about the Youngbloods. He shows up maybe once a month or so, but his wife and Lucinda are there every Sunday."

"Folks in town come out this way?"

"Yup. Way back when, the Chances reckoned the time had come for Reliable to have a real church building. Before then, folks came and worshipped in our yard if the weather was fair. On bad days, we held church in the barn. The plot of land where the road forks between our place and the MacPhersons' seemed logical."

"Are there as many MacPhersons as there are Chances?"

"More.

"Most every place I've been, there are a few big families that run the community." He held up one hand. "I didn't mean that in a bad way. Communities need leaders."

"Reliable isn't all that big, but plenty of folks step up when things need doing. The Dorseys' barn burned last year. Everyone pitched in, and a new one was up the next week."

"Turning tragedy into good."

Tanner shrugged. "Not that big of a disaster. Tragedy—well, the Walls' wagon overturned a year back. Lost all of 'em 'cept for the father. Don't see much of him these days."

Matt tried to sound casual as he asked, "Anyone know what started the barn fire?"

"Never know about those things."

Stills sometimes blew up. That could explain the fire. Feigning an absence of any real curiosity, Matt shrugged. "Dumb question. Accidents just happen—like that wagon flipping over."

Tanner's features tightened. "That accident shouldn't have ever happened."

Holding his hands up in front of himself, Matt shook his head. "Whoa. Sorry if I hit a nerve. Chance Ranch's horses are the finest I've ever seen. If the horse—"

"Wasn't the horse." Tanner's features twisted with disgust. "Thaddeus Walls was drunk as a skunk when it happened."

Matt whistled under his breath.

"The Good Book tells us not to judge. But it would be a far sight easier for me to pity Thad if I didn't remember his wife's weeping. Since our place was closest, they brought Etta here. Doc, Polly, and Aunt Lovejoy did their best. It wasn't enough. I've always reckoned Etta didn't want to live anymore—not without her children." Tanner looked away. "We've got this section done."

Understanding the topic had closed, Matt grinned. "Good. I'm hankering after those sandwiches Kate sent with us."

"Me, too. Sis is a fair cook."

"Fair? I've relished everything she's made."

Tanner smacked him on the back. "That's 'cuz you've been eating your own food too long."

"Anything beats my cooking." Matt opened the small knapsack and drew out a stack of sandwiches wrapped in a dishcloth. "But I know good cooking when I taste it."

❧

"This is a disaster!" Kate slammed the lid back down on the roasting pan and resisted the urge to kick the stove. She wanted to impress Matthew Salter with her cooking; one look at this burned roast, and he was liable to hop on his horse and head for the hills.

"No, it's not." April motioned to her to lift the lid. "Plunk the roast down over here, then put on some rice to cook."

"Why?"

"Because," April smiled, "no one's going to know it got burnt. While the rice is boiling, you'll trim off the crispy edges of the roast, then chop the good meat into bite-sized pieces. We'll use the drippings to make gravy and—"

Kate stood stock-still in the middle of the kitchen, holding the roast precariously aloft with a big carving knife. "You mean the times you make beef and rice. . .it's because you. . ."

Her cousin winked. "Now let's get busy. I'll put the evidence in the slop bucket and cover it with a splash of milk."

"I can't believe it," Kate crowed about half an hour later. "Dinner's going to turn out fine."

Laughing, April nodded. "Plenty can go wrong in the kitchen. If the fire in the stove burns too hot or too cool, even the best recipe fails. The trick is learning how to recover from a disaster. Often what you make out of the mess is just as good, if not better, than what you started with."

"I haven't decided what to take for dessert to the picnic tomorrow." Kate set two bowls heaping with snap beans on the table. April promptly dabbed butter on them.

"What about taking—"

"Hey, sis!" Tobias hollered from outside. "I'm half-starved. Is supper ready?"

Normally, Kate would have yelled back her answer, but now that seemed. . .well, not very ladylike. She walked to the doorway, pushed open the screen, and stepped out onto the porch. "If you're only half-starved, you must've had a snack thirty minutes ago."

The Chance men all chuckled. Even so, Kate heard a deep, rumbling laugh that didn't belong to her brothers or cousins. She turned and spied Matthew Salter. Glee sparkled in his brown eyes. She smiled back at him. "Supper's ready. T's grab the dishes. P's, take the food."

"Miss Chance, I'm an M." Matthew drew closer. "What's my chore?"

"Mr. Salter—"

"Looks like a mighty capable dishwasher to me!" Paxton declared, slapping the ranch hand on the back.

The opportunity to shuffle around the sink and cupboard with Mr. Salter sounded heavenly. Still, saddling a man with that chore didn't often happen around Chance Ranch. Kate opened her mouth, but Matt spoke first.

"On one condition. You call me Matt, not Mr. Salter."

Someone whooped in the kitchen, then bellowed, "Beef and rice!"

Kate shifted to the side to avoid being trampled.

Caleb started through the doorway. Tobias and Tanner pushed past him, exiting the cabin with heaping plates. Tanner yelled, "It's every man for himself!"

Matt shouldered through the line and grabbed their plates. "Ladies first, of course. Thanks for thinking of the gals. Miss Kate and Miss April, I'll set this food on the table for you."

Tanner and Tobias exchanged outraged looks, then plowed back toward the kitchen.

April came around the cabin holding a plate with a modest helping of supper and a pitcher full of gravy. "It's worse than a stampede in there. The men are so food-crazed, they've plumb forgotten the cabin has a back door they can use to exit!"

Looking at the two plates in Matt's hands, Kate's heart did a funny little flip. "Well, Mr.—I mean, Matt—it looks as if you've avoided the throng and still ended up with supper."

"Brings that saying to mind. 'All good things come to those who wait.'" He set a plate on the picnic table, then looked at her and said in a low voice, "Some things are especially worth waiting for."

All through supper, Kate told herself he'd been referring to the meal. *Maybe he meant me, too. How am I to know? Laurel would have known. She had suitors fighting over her.*

"Kate, what's wrong?" Packard frowned at her. "Are you sick?"

"No. Why?"

"You just poured gravy on your beans."

"It's my fault!" April half shouted.

All of the men stopped staring at Kate and turned toward her cousin. Blushing, April muttered, "I didn't put enough butter on them." She jerked her chin upward. "As a matter of fact, I'd like to put gravy on my beans, too."

Matt cleared his throat. "Best gravy I ever tasted. If there's any left, I wouldn't mind trying it on my beans, too."

Kate appreciated how her cousin spoke out. Bless her heart, April knew exactly how to divert the men's attention so they wouldn't figure out Kate was so enamored of the new ranch hand that she'd lost track of what she was doing. But Matt? Why had he chimed in? *Men. I've been surrounded by them all my life—outnumbered by them—but I don't understand them. Especially this new hand. . .but I'd like to figure him out!*

"Hey, sis." Tanner passed the gravy boat to Matt. "Barbed wire sprang back today. Ripped Matt's work glove. Think you can stitch it up?"

"I'd be happy to take a look at it."

Caleb leaned forward and demanded, "Neither of you got cut, did you?"

"Nah," Tanner said. "Woulda sliced my chest something awful if Matt didn't have such fast reflexes, though."

"You would have done the same for me," Matt said. He then looked at Kate. "It's kind of you to offer to take a look at my glove, but your sewing needles won't begin to pierce leather."

Packard burst out cackling.

Tanner grinned. "Kate does all of the leatherwork for Chance Ranch."

Matt's brow furrowed.

Kate's heart dropped. *Tobias told me it's not a ladylike pursuit. What is Matt going to think?*

nine

"Your parents named you Tanner, but you don't work leather?"

Tanner chuckled. "Never thought about it before."

Kate fought the urge to put down her fork and bury her stained hands in her lap.

"And you," Matt turned his gaze on her, "you made the belts your brothers and cousins wear?"

She nodded stiffly.

"Saddles, too," Caleb chimed in.

April giggled. "You don't wear saddles!"

"Some days, I think they ought to." Kate bit her lip once she'd blurted out that statement.

Tobias bumped her with his arm as he shrugged. "At least she didn't say muzzles."

While everyone else at the table chuckled, Matt didn't. He continued to stare at her. Kate couldn't read the look in his deep brown eyes. The rest of the meal, Matt didn't say much. Kate took a few more bites and set down her fork.

"Whats'a matter?" Tobias focused on her plate.

"I'm not hungry."

"Sure you're not turning sick?"

Lovesick. "I'm fine."

"We both tasted the food while cooking." April pushed her plate away. "I've had all I'm going to eat, too."

While their brothers swooped over and swiped the rest of their food, Kate gave April a smile of gratitude. *April knows I'm fond of Matt, and twice tonight she's kept me from making a fool of myself. Beef and rice is one of her favorites, and she's going*

78

hungry just to help me.

A short while later, with bubbles surrounding his muscular forearms, Matt grinned at Kate as she dried a plate. "Not much to wash, really. Supper tasted so good, I fought the temptation to lick my plate. Your brothers and cousins scraped every last grain of rice off theirs, too."

"I'm glad you liked it." Kate shot April a look. "It's April's recipe. Compared to how she cooks, what I make is only fit for slopping the hogs."

"I haven't tasted Miss April's cooking, but I'm still going to disagree." He felt around in the bottom of the water and pulled out one last spoon. "Speaking of hog slop, do you add the dishwater to it?"

"I'll do it!" Kate set down the plate so fast, it almost cracked.

"Actually, I need to add a little cornmeal first." April bustled over and grabbed a scoop. "Especially since we didn't add any dinner scraps, the hogs'll need this. Kate, why don't you pour in that last bit of milk, then let Mr. Salter use the pitcher to dip out the dishwater?"

"Good idea."

Matt cleared his throat. "I mean no familiarity, but I'd rather be called Matt. It was part of the deal Miss Kate and I made when I offered to wash the dishes."

"It doesn't seem equitable for us to call you Matt and have you use 'Miss' in front of our given names." April kept stirring cornmeal into the slop and tacked on, "Don't you agree, Kate?"

"Absolutely."

Matt shook his head. "My mama drilled a few things into my thick head, and she'd be spinning in her grave if I lost my manners at all, especially around ladies. I'd be making a false promise if I said I'd address either of you in such a way. I reckon the only woman I'll ever call simply by her first name is the gal I'll wed."

Oh. He's just as much as said he's not interested in me. And why would he be? Tobias was right—men don't want women who are boisterous and disheveled.

"You can add in the milk and dishwater now." April stepped back. "By the way, Kate, Peter needs laces for his boots. Do you think you could make him a pair?"

Kate nodded.

Once Matt added the dishwater to the slop, he lifted the heavy bucket. "I spied the pigpen on the far side of the barn."

"I'll take this." Kate tried to pull on the handle.

"No, you won't. No reason for a woman to tote when a man's willing to help her out. Besides. . ." He paused, and a smile tugged at the right side of his mouth. "I'm trying to come up with an excuse to talk you into showing me your workshop."

"I already said I'd repair the tear in your glove."

"And I'd be much obliged. Now you turn loose of this slop bucket, Miss Kate."

"Kate isn't sure she ought to let you near Frenzy." April looked down at her hands and frowned at the blisters. "I'd be happy to do the chore, myself, but—"

"You wouldn't dare. Doc and Polly would have a fit!"

Matt chortled. "They'd have to stand in line behind Peter."

"But Frenzy," April said woefully. "She's been in a wicked temper for days now. She's our meanest sow. Kate, you'd better go along. Make sure the gate to the pen isn't loose. You know how the lock's slipped the last few days."

"You ladies oughtn't fret over such a thing. I'll be sure to repair that at once."

"Thank you." April looked entirely too pleased with herself. "Kate's workbench is in the stable, and the men keep all of the woodworking tools just to the right of her place."

Thousands of times, Kate had walked beside a man—her father, uncles, brothers, and cousins. But walking through the barnyard with Matt felt different. His loose-hipped gait testified to years spent in the saddle, and the square set of his shoulders showed confidence that he could handle whatever life threw his way. He switched the slop bucket to his left hand, away from her. Kate couldn't tell whether he'd done so to put the smelly thing farther away from her or if it was so Matt could walk a little closer.

He looked down at her, and his brows rose in silent query.

Kate didn't want to tell him what she'd been wondering, so she blurted out, "How did you know about giving the hogs dishwater?"

Matt hitched his shoulder. "I thought most everybody knew the lye in the water cured hogs of worms. Now that I think it over, I'm not sure when I learned about that fact. Growing up around animals, those bits of wisdom are passed on."

Whew. So he didn't think I'm crass for asking such a dumb question. "So you grew up around animals—farm or ranch?"

"A little horse ranch. Nothing near as splendid as this spread."

"Where?" She winced. "Sorry. I'm prying."

"Nothing wrong with asking simple questions. Wyoming. My dad was the foreman. Worked solid, made the place turn a profit for the widow-woman who owned the spread."

"Why leave a place like that?"

"The widow up and married. Her husband didn't want someone else giving orders." He stopped at the pen. "You'd best step back, Miss Kate. No use risking you getting splattered when I pour this into the trough."

"I'm already a wreck."

Matt looked her from neckline to hem and back again. Shaking his head, he murmured, "I disagree. You look like a woman who's not afraid to work hard for her family."

"I—" Horrified, she stammered, "I wasn't fishing for a compliment, Matt."

"I know." He grinned. "Life's taught me women don't seek praise on their appearance unless they're dead certain every last bow and flounce is perfect."

She looked down at her smudged apron and the dust-covered hem of her rose calico dress, then forced a laugh. "Not a single bow." *Oh, no! I hope he doesn't think I meant beau!*

"Some men admire gals who prance around like live fashion plates. Me? I'd ruther see a woman whose smile warms a man to the toe of his boots and whose rumpled apron bespeaks a willingness to pitch in alongside her loved ones." He pivoted and poured the slop into the trough. "*Sooo-eeeEEE! Sooo-eeeEEE!* Pig, pig, pig, pig!"

The hogs squealed and trampled through the muck. Matt chuckled. "I didn't need to call them, did I?"

"No, but you might win a hog-calling contest. Your pitch is great." Kate giggled.

"What's so funny?"

"Promise you won't tell?"

He lifted one foot and rested his boot on the first slat of the pen. "I like to know what I'm giving my word about. If it's illegal or unethical, I couldn't agree."

"I was thinking. . ." She laughed again. "My brothers looked just like that, pushing into the kitchen for supper tonight!"

Amusement lit his eyes and lifted the corners of his mouth. "Can't say as I blame them. Had I known chow was that tasty, I might have jostled my way to the head of the line."

❧

Giggles spilled out of Kate. They weren't the practiced twitters of young ladies who played coy. Hers were so honest and refreshing, Matt was thoroughly enchanted. He didn't want to walk her back to the house yet, so he decided to string the conversation along on a topic she could speak about with ease. "So you do leatherwork." Something flashed in Kate's eyes, but

Matt didn't know how to read it. "Never seen such handsome belts. You do quality work."

"Thank you." She glanced over her shoulder.

"Nice diversionary tactic, that glance." Matt reached over and gently tugged on her sleeve. "But you don't have to hide your hands behind your back."

She let out a small sound of despair.

Curling his fingers around the cuff of her sleeve, he drew her hands out in the open. "It's just stain, isn't it?"

Kate nodded. "Yes." Her chin went up a notch. "I'm more splotched than not."

"I disagree." He flashed her a smile. "I'd say you're more not than splotched. Besides, what does that matter?"

"It's ugly. Not very ladylike, either."

That same fleeting look crossed her face, and Matt realized she'd just revealed her vulnerability. "I disagree. The stain on your hands is only skin-deep. The devotion you show to your family by doing that fine work is soul-deep. To my way of thinking, nothing's more beautiful than a woman who loves with all her heart."

Her eyes widened, and a flush of pleasure tinted her cheeks. Funny, how something so inconsequential mattered so much to women. But Matt was glad the truth he'd spoken made her feel good. He looked down at the empty pail. "I'll rinse this and set it out on the back porch."

"You don't need to do that."

"No reason why I shouldn't. No job is beneath a man's dignity—that's what my granddad always said."

"He sounds like a wise man."

"He never had more than two years' schooling, but Grand-dad was blessed with wisdom that came from the Lord."

"Kate?" They turned in tandem toward Paxton's voice. "When you make the bootlaces for Peter, make an extra length."

"How long?"

Not why, but how long? Matt noted how she just took it as a matter of course that the requested item was needed and didn't demand a reason.

"Not all that long. Maybe eight inches." Paxton scuffed the toe of his boots in the dirt as a guilty flush colored his cheeks. "I broke the loop on the fishing basket."

"You went fishing without me?"

Matt couldn't be sure whether Kate was outraged or teasing. She wasn't like any other woman he'd ever met.

Heaving a sigh, Paxton kicked the dirt. "Didn't go for long. It was a waste of time. Nothing was biting, unless you count mosquitoes."

"I have a scrap of leather that'll yield a thong long enough to do the repair. Here. Go rinse out the swill bucket and bring me the fishing basket."

"Salter—"

"Offered to fix the gate on the pigpen," Kate cut in. "I'll show him where the tools are since I'm heading toward my workbench."

Paxton accepted the smelly bucket. "Watch out for Frenzy. She's the runty-looking sow. Her name warns you of her temperament."

"Obliged for the warning."

Paxton stared at Kate and smirked. "Ever notice how the little ones are always the scrappiest?"

"Nothing wrong with having plenty of spark and spirit. Miss Kate, do I need to fetch a lantern from the kitchen for you so you'll have light to work by?"

She shook her head. "There's one on either end of my workbench. You can have one if you think it'll take long to fix the latch."

"Doubt that'll be necessary." He walked alongside her

toward the far side of the barn. Kate's gait matched her personality—her zest for life showed not only in her bright eyes and friendly smile, but in her high-stepping prance that made her sway and bob as though she heard a lively march and couldn't resist matching the rhythm.

Sliding the barn door wide open, Matt asked, "Ever do custom pieces for neighbors and friends?"

She headed toward a cluttered table that had a pair of well-ordered shelves above it. "Sure. I've often made gifts for them."

He drew near and took the matches from her. She could have easily lit the lantern herself, but Matt didn't like a woman doing things for herself when he could do them—especially Kate. From the moment he'd arrived, she'd been in motion, always doing things for others. It wouldn't hurt for someone to show her the same kindness.

The match sizzled, then Matt held it to the wick as Kate held up the hurricane glass. The wick caught, and Kate settled the glass sleeve in place. Matt reached up and barely grazed her left cheekbone.

"It's not stain. Really, it isn't."

"I'm partial to freckles." He stepped back. What was it about Kate that had him acting this way? He'd never dallied with a gal's affection, and he wasn't about to—but this was different. Kate was different. *But I can't be completely honest with her. I'm on assignment, and I have a job to do. If the rest of the family is as forthright and upright as everyone I've already met, I'm going to need to move on to continue my search.*

I don't want to move on.

But I do. It would tear Kate apart to learn someone she loves is involved in bootlegging.

"Probably all you need are a nail or two and the hammer." She waved toward the nearby tool bench. "Just be careful. Pax wasn't kidding when he said Frenzy riles easily."

The latch on the pen turned out to be quite sturdy once Matt moved it up an inch. Someone else had reinforced it previously, so the nail holes were too large to anchor the latch in the same location. As he placed the hammer back into the spot he'd taken it from on the tool bench, Matt let out a low whistle.

Kate's hands stopped. "What?"

"You've already almost finished that lace?" He gazed at the long leather thong hanging from her fingers.

She hitched her left shoulder diffidently. "This is the second one. They don't take all that long. I cut a circle, then just keep cutting spiral-style into it."

"That knife has to be sharp. I'd massacre the leather and my hands."

"I've cut myself on occasion." She started working again and tacked on, "More often in the kitchen than by working leather."

"Beats me why you talk like that. Every last meal I've eaten here has tasted mighty fine, and you've been the cook."

Kate shrugged. "I can turn out a passable meal. Once you taste April's fare, you'll understand."

"Not that good food isn't high up in my estimation, but a meal is gone in a short while. The saddles and belts you make last for years."

"Ah, but the latch on the fishing basket didn't." She set down the bootlace, bent over a scrap of leather, and carefully scribed a circle on it.

He didn't want to leave. Talking with Kate counted as a pure pleasure. Then, too, he hoped to glean some information from her. Matt leaned against her workbench. "I've seen the stuff you've made here on Chance Ranch. Tell me about what you've made for neighbors."

"Mrs. Dorsey had me make her husband a saddle to replace the one he lost in their barn fire. My family voted to give them all of the spare halters, leads, and the like that we had on hand."

"That's the second time you've mentioned voting."

"It's a family rule: Anyone in the family who's twenty-one is given the right to vote on issues."

"I don't mean to be indelicate, but you're not of voting age—at least, that's what I gathered when Caleb, Tanner, and April were speaking the other night."

"I'm not." She tilted her head to the side and continued to cut the leather thong.

"So everyone older than you voted to give away the work you'd done."

"Never thought of it that way. Chances share. It would be miserly of us to keep halters and such that we don't even use when a neighbor is in need."

"I agree. So tell me about your other neighbors."

"You've already met Peter and Johnna. They're from the MacPherson spread. Tomorrow, we'll have a family picnic after church. You—"

"Sis?" Tanner moseyed into the workshop and shoved his hands into his pockets. "What're you doing?"

"Making bootlaces for Peter. Why?"

"Just wondered." Tanner pulled his hands back out of his pockets and pulled a knife from his belt sheath. "Reckoned I ought to make more clothespins. I don't think we have nearly enough."

"Probably not." She turned her attention back to Matt. "Anyway, you're welcome to go to church with us tomorrow; then we have the picnic afterward."

"I already asked him."

"Appreciate the invitation. It'll be good to worship." Though he felt strongly about the necessity of Christian fellowship, Matt wished Tanner would saunter off. At the present, spending time with Kate—only Kate—sounded far more appealing.

"MacPhersons are coming here for the picnic," Kate said as she finished the piece she'd started.

"We swap." Tanner examined the small block of wood he'd picked up, then dragged a stool over closer to the lantern. "Once or twice a month we have a family get-together."

"Judging from how Peter and April act, I'd say the family ties are going to grow stronger."

Kate flashed him a smile. "Isn't it wonderful? I'm so happy for her."

"I'm not." Tanner smirked as he hiked up his pantleg and slid onto the stool. "Well, I am, but I don't think we ought to let her marry and move away until she teaches you more of her special recipes."

"Kate'll move away when she marries, too."

Tanner let out a snort. "No danger of that."

ten

Kate blushed so deeply, her freckles completely disappeared.

Matt lounged against her worktable. "You might be right. A man could get lost in her pretty blue eyes and decide to marry her and stay right here on Chance Ranch."

Tanner's head flew up, but the surprised look on his face immediately changed. "Ouch!"

Kate slipped off her stool and fished a hanky from her apron pocket. "Here."

Matt marveled that Kate ignored her brother's ridicule and tended his cut. Most people would have gloated and said it served him right.

"No use in getting that bloodstained." Tanner plucked a bandana from his pocket.

"Oh, no." Kate yanked the bandana away and shoved it onto her worktable. "That has to be dirtier than Methuselah's tent."

"Methuselah's tent?" Matt echoed, thoroughly entertained by her choice of words.

Kate held her hanky against Tanner's finger. "If that amuses you, you're going to have fun tomorrow."

"Yeah, he will."

"Why?"

"The MacPherson brothers hail from Hawk's Fall, Kentucky. They got so lonely, so they went to a neighboring place in Kentucky called Salt Lake Holler for brides. Tempy's sister Lovejoy came as the brides' chaperone. Our uncle Daniel snagged her for himself. All of that being said, they brought a rich heritage and delightfully colorful speech with them."

Many of those Appalachian men are adept at brewing moonshine. It's part of their culture, and the land there isn't rich enough to support a family. More than a few of those people earn their living by operating a still.

Kate slowly peeled away the handkerchief, then pressed it back around her brother's finger. "You need to go wash this with lye soap."

"No need to fuss over it." Tanner scowled at her.

Kate pretended not to hear him. "After you do, sprinkle some styptic powder over it."

"Hey, what's going on in here?" Tobias came in, carrying the fishing basket. He set it on Kate's worktable. "Pax said this needs fixing."

"Tanner's going to go take care of his finger. He cut it. I'm going to fix the basket."

"It's nothing." Tanner curled his hand around the reddening hanky. "Just a little slice."

Tobias's brows knit. "How'd you—"

"Whittling."

"Go take care of that." Tobias bumped his brother off the stool, then took the perch for himself and picked up the same block of wood. "I'll take care of this."

This? Matt hooked one boot heel on the workbench's crossbar. *The clothespins are just an excuse to stick around out here so Kate isn't alone with me. It's no wonder no one's courted and married her—she has half an army of brothers and cousins to be sure a man can't get close to her.*

Unwilling to be put off, Matt grabbed another block of wood. "What kind of clothespins are we making?"

Tobias chuckled softly. He stood and reached for a large tin bucket on Kate's upper shelf. As he set it down, dozens upon dozens of homemade clothespins rattled inside. Flipping one to Matt, Tobias said, "This kind."

Matt ran his thumb along the wooden piece. "I didn't know anyone still whittled these. You can buy factory-made ones for a song."

"Aunt Lovejoy believes if you can't make something for yourself, you don't need it." Tobias shaved off a corner of the wood.

That explained why. Still, Matt didn't understand why they were making more. "Not to dismiss the virtue of work, but it looks to me like you've already made plenty."

"Gifts should always be from the heart." As soon as the words slipped out of her mouth, Kate bit her lip and cast a questioning look at her older brother.

Intrigued by the small mystery, Matt prodded, "So the clothespins are gifts?"

"You've let the cat out of the bag," Tobias muttered.

"I'm sorry." She bowed her head.

"It's not a big deal. No use getting upset over it." Tobias looked at Matt. "On his ninth birthday, every Chance is given a knife. He's taught to whittle—mostly little animals and toys. Same with the MacPhersons."

"So you exchange gifts?"

Tobias shook his head. "Not those things."

Matt knew when someone was trying to deflect questions by redirecting the conversation. He'd learned to string them along as though he was fooled, then when they let down their guard, he'd go right back and discover what they were trying to hide. "Then where do the toys go?"

Some of the tension in Kate's shoulders and in Tobias's jaw eased. Kate said, "They go to children who wouldn't otherwise have toys."

He took up a knife and started on one of the rectangular wooden blocks. "There's a wonderful orphanage in San Francisco. If you don't have anyone or any place specific in mind,

I'm sure they'd appreciate having toys for the little ones."

Kate concentrated as she repaired the fishing basket. "We could keep that in mind, couldn't we, Tobias?"

"Reckon we could—but there have to be at least a couple of orphanages in such a big city."

"The one I have in mind is unique. It's an enormous old mansion. Most of the younger children are adopted quite quickly, and the older ones receive educations or training in keeping with their talents so they can be self-reliant when they leave."

Squinting at the wood in his hands, Tobias said, "Our mother grew up in an orphanage."

"She must be a special woman to have married into this family and reared you as she has."

"Mama is very special." Kate straightened up and patted the fishing basket. "There. Good as new."

Knowing he had to press for answers or lose this opportunity, Matt's gaze went from Kate to her brother and back. "The two of you are dodging my question as to what happens to the clothespins."

Kate's shoulders drooped. "You know how in the Bible it exhorts us to give without the other hand knowing? It's one of those situations."

"I can respect that."

"Good." Tobias's curt tone made it clear he thought the discussion was over.

"I've seen some that were all painted and decorated to serve as Christmas ornaments." Matt held his up toward the light and pretended to squint along the side to see if it was smooth. Though Kate didn't make a sound, he sensed her sudden inhalation. *So that's why they're sensitive.* "I reckon there aren't all that many things you can do with clothespins." He went back to whittling. "If you're worried I'm opposed to Christmas trees, I'm not. I figure Christ is like an evergreen—His beauty refreshes us and gives us life. Then, too, it never depends on the seasons of life—His love endures even through the coldest, darkest times."

"That's quite a testimonial." Tobias grinned. "So are you coming to church with us tomorrow?"

Kate laughed. "Tanner invited him, then I invited him. Now you did."

"And they also invited me to go to the picnic."

Looking at his sister, Tobias asked, "Did you tell him about the MacPhersons' dishes?"

"Not yet."

"Don't." An impish smile tugged at the corners of Tobias's mouth.

"I overheard Johnna saying something to Peter about cat-head biscuits. If that's the kind of food they bring, I'm going to make a pig of myself."

"You did that at supper tonight." Tobias's grin bloomed.

"It's Kate's fault. She cooks better food than I've ever eaten."

"I've told him to wait until April is back at the stove."

"You've been whippin' up some decent meals on your own, sis. What're you making for the picnic?"

"I've already made Aunt Miriam's coleslaw. It's hanging in the well along with egg salad, and I boiled potatoes for potato salad. While I make that tonight, I'll bake some shoofly pie. I have some lemons that need to be used up. Maybe I'll do a lemon meringue, too."

"Now you've done it." Matt gave her a baleful look.

"What did I do?"

"Lemon pie. I'll lie in bed thinking about it, and come morning, when there's not a trace left of that lemon pie, I'll be fired. Instead of going to church, I'll be heading down the road, searching for a new job."

Kate's eyes sparkled with merriment. "You could still go to

church. It's the perfect place for sinners to repent."

"Now there's the problem. I couldn't say I was one bit sorry for what I'd done."

"Better make a couple lemon meringues." Tobias stretched. "I might have to supervise our new hand if he takes to wandering around at night."

"If you eat that much, when folks talk about the Chance spread, no one will know whether they're discussing you or the ranch."

"I have a long way to go before I look like Mr. Roland."

Matt jumped on the opportunity. "Roland. Now there's a neighbor you haven't mentioned yet. So what does he do?"

"Eat," Tobias said succinctly.

"He's turned his cattle operation over to his son and his son-in-law." Kate opened and shut the basket lid a few times to assure herself everything lined up easily. "Gout's made it hard for him to get around much. I can understand why he's thickened in the middle a bit."

"Must be a huge holding if he's got two men running it."

"Just average-sized, but Sam and Hector are doing something right because it appears they're turning a tidy profit."

So they might have found another way to make money—and moonshining is lucrative.

"Speaking of the picnic. . ." Kate methodically put away the few tools she'd used. "I was so busy with supper, I forgot to tell you that April and Peter invited the Youngbloods to come."

"Great!" Tobias deftly started creating the center notch in his clothespin. "Guess that means we'll have to leave that lemon pie alone tonight, Salter. Lucinda's real fond of them."

"You men can stay here and whittle to your hearts' content. I need to get back to the kitchen."

Matt regretted that Kate had to leave—even more than he regretted her big brother barging in and playing chaperon. *I'll manage to spend time with her tomorrow at the picnic. Meantime, maybe I can get Tobias to tell me more about the folks around here.*

"Tanner said just about everyone attends church. That's good to hear. Most towns have a couple of skeptics or black sheep. . . ."

❧

"No. No thank you." Lucinda looked up at Tobias and batted her eyes. "You're a big man. You eat it for me."

Peter tossed a pickle onto his plate. Lucinda made a big to-do over what she'd eat. For coming here without a single dish to share, it seemed mighty wrong for her to be so finicky. Then again, her mother had taken one look at the womenfolk putting out the huge spread of food and suddenly declared she felt poorly. Mr. Youngblood took her on home.

Peter plopped down close to April. "Here. Have a bite." He held the sandwich up for her. He'd used the excuse of her sore hands to make them eat off the same plate.

"Oh! It's your mama's chicken salad!"

Mama beamed. "I made it special, jist for you, lamb."

April took a bite, closed her eyes as she relished the flavor, and swallowed. "Magnificent! Thank you for making it."

"Thangs keep a-headin' where they are betwixt you and my son, I'll wind up sharin' my secret recipe with you right soon."

Turning the same shade as the inside of a ripe watermelon, April swiped a pickle off the plate and took a big bite. Her face twisted in dismay.

Lord, ever'body else knows we're a good match. Why's April actin' like this?

She dropped the rest of the pickle back onto the plate and shook her hand in the air. A small sound of distress curled in her throat.

"Peter, pour yore water o'er her fingers. That salty brine's hurting her dreadful."

He emptied his cup over April's hand, then accepted Matt Salter's. After pouring it slowly over the blisters that had opened, Peter yanked a bandana from his pocket and gently dried her fingers. "That any better, honey pie?"

A choppy sigh accompanied a tiny bob of her head.

"Best you go on a-feedin' her," Pa declared.

Johnna chimed in, "Yep. Hit'll be good practice for when you give her a bite from yore weddin' cake."

Still red as could be, April called back over to his sister, "Don't go rushing things. You and Trevor have been courting well over a year. If anyone's due to marry, it's you!"

"He's fixin' to ask her," one of his little cousins shouted.

"Hush," Mama chided.

"But I'm only tellin' the truth. I heard Trevor talkin' to Uncle Obie. He asked—"

Aunt Eunice clapped her hand over her son's mouth. "You done said more'n 'nuff."

Trevor chortled. Fishing something out of his shirt pocket, he shifted onto his knees. "Johnna, I planned to take you off on a walk all alone, but since I'm getting so much help, I'll ask you here and now." He pulled out a ring. "I love you. Will you marry me?"

While they kissed, everyone cheered.

Matt Salter frowned. "Shouldn't she give him her answer?"

"Already did," Peter declared. "MacPhersons don't kiss unless they're bespoken."

"Hey, Peter!" Trevor called over. He shot a meaningful look at April. "Jump on in. The water's fine!"

Caleb shouted back, "Not a chance!"

Paxton let out a whoop. "That's right. April won't be a Chance anymore."

Peter looked at April. A fetching blush stained her cheeks, and she bit her lower lip—something she rarely did. *Nothing would make me happier than to propose here and now, but she's not ready yet. She deserves a full courtship and to know how deep my love flows ere I ask her.* Peter lifted his chin and gave her a slow, audacious wink.

Caleb cleared his throat loudly. "Nobody's doing any proposing to anyone until our folks get home."

"That's only proper," Kate agreed. She smiled and tacked on, "Our folks are due home late this week."

"That gladdens my heart," Aunt Tempy said. "I've missed my sister more than words can tell."

"I'm sure Aunt Lovejoy's missed you every bit as much." April sighed. "I've worried about her."

"Frettin' ne'er yields good." Ma caught little Matilda as she toddled by and started to tie her shoe. "We'll all hold our Lovejoy up to Jesus."

"Thank you, Aunt Lois." April gave Peter's mother a tender smile. "I've been thinking about you all going to Yosemite the next few summers. While you're praying, I want you to ask the Lord about leaving Matilda in my care. Aunt Eunice, I'd keep Elvera for you, too. That way, you'd all be able to enjoy yourselves more."

"Ain't that kind of you!" Aunt Eunice said as she poked a tomato wedge into Elvera's mouth.

Ma gave Matilda a hug, and Matilda gave her a sloppy baby kiss before pushing away and coming straight to Peter. She curled her chubby little fingers around the other part of the pickle. "Pees?"

April pulled his tiny sister down into her lap. "Yes, but you have to sit down here to eat. No running around with food in yore mouth."

"I can watch the young'uns," Johnna said. "I already went to Yosemite."

"Nope." Trevor nestled her close. "I aim to go see Yosemite.

I want my bride by my side."

A deep longing speared through Peter. *I want the woman by my side to be my bride.*

"Kate?" April tugged on her cousin's sash. "Don't you think Johnna ought to come to our cabin to make her wedding gown?"

Kate bobbed her head. "We have plenty of room, and it can be left out instead of being tucked away when you can't work on it."

Ma sighed. "I always reckoned my daughters would wear my weddin' dress. But yore a whole hand taller. I checked the hem last night, and it's not deep 'nuff to let down for you, Johnna."

"Lambkins, could be one of the others'll still wear it." Pa patted Ma's shoulder. "I'll send Peter to San Francisco to fetch a dress length of fine satin. That way, that gal of ourn cain stitch a purdy dress she cain pass on to her own daughter someday."

Matilda twisted and held up the end of the pickle she'd been gnawing on for April to have a bite. April pretended to nibble on it. "Mmm-mmm! Thank you!" She turned to Peter. "Laurel and Gabe are in Boston, visiting his family."

Lucinda fluffed up row upon row of ruffles in her skirts. "Mama has all of my clothes made back East."

"No daughter of mine's gonna walk down the aisle in a ready-made gown." Ma shook her head. "I won't have it."

Lucinda spluttered. "My dresses are not ready made!"

"Yore right purdy in that frock, Lucy." Ma reached for her mug of water.

Peter was glad she did, because she missed seeing Lucinda's scowl. He didn't know whether Tobias's sweetheart didn't accept the heartfelt compliment or if she objected to Ma's habit of granting folks nicknames. Either way, the gal oughtn't be so disrespectful to her elders.

Ma kept on talking. "Yes, you are a sight to behold. But ever' stitch in a weddin' gown ought to be made with hope and prayer, not by a machine. Machines don't carry a thread of love."

"Making Polly and Laurel's dresses was so much fun," Kate said.

"Plenty of love and joy filled the hours we spent." April looked at Peter. "We could send a telegram and have Laurel ship material to San Francisco."

"Won't that be expensive?" Lucinda stared at her plate and scooted the food around.

Peter bristled. *She'd best mind her tongue. Just 'cuz we MacPhersons ain't wealthy don't mean we don't do right by our own.*

"It won't be expensive at all." April beamed. Bless her heart, it never occurred to her that someone might be unkind. "Laurel and Gabe took a list from us before they left. Laurel already told me she planned to send back fabric for the MacPherson clan. We didn't ask what you'd like—"

"Because you always wear golden yellow," Kate said.

Johnna burst out, "I don't want a yeller weddin' dress."

"But you'd look gorgeous carrying yellow flowers." April lovingly rubbed her cheek against Matilda's mop of russet curls.

Peter's heart swelled. April cherished his kin. Here she was, natural as breathing, lovin' on his sisters. Everyone in both families knew for certain that he'd fallen head-over-heels in love with her—everyone but her. *Someday soon, she'll see the truth.*

"I'd never carry yellow roses." Lucinda stuck her nose in the air. "They represent infidelity."

The friendly chatter came to a dead halt.

Trevor curled his arm tightly around Johnna. "Johnna and me—our love is stronger than that sort of nonsense."

"Some of those customs have no meaning here," Tobias told Lucinda.

"That's right." Johnna smoothed her hand down her yellow gown. "I reckon I wouldn't much feel like myself iff'n I didn't have yeller somewheres on my weddin' day."

"It doesn't matter what you hold in your hand," April said. "It's what you hold in your heart. We all know how devoted you are to one another."

Matt Salter rose. "Anyone need anything?"

"I couldn't possibly eat another morsel." Lucinda's gaze shifted toward April. "Gluttony is a sin."

eleven

"Pride's a sin," Peter half-growled.

"And sloth," Kate chimed in.

"That leaves greed, envy, wrath, and. . ." Tanner's brows knit.

"Lust," Pa finished. "Mr. Salter, iff'n yore headin' to the table, I'd appreciate you toting back some of that Heinz ketchup."

Matt nodded. "Sure will. I'm getting more of that noodle stuff if any's left."

Tanner chortled. "You like it, huh?"

"Delicious."

"Coupla rattlers got bold and slithered into the henhouse," Pa said.

Ma nodded. "Eunice skinned them snakes and boiled up a mess of noodles."

"So you've been eating rattler!" Tanner's eyes danced with mirth.

Lucinda shoved her plate to the side and started gagging. She scrambled off the blanket and raced toward a clump of trees.

Salter shrugged. "Isn't the first time I've had rattler. Hope it's not the last. I'd rather eat snake than have one take a bite of me any day."

Kate started to get up. "I suppose I ought to go see if Lucinda needs any help."

"Thanks, sis." Tobias handed her his bandana.

"Bring over a cup of water in a few minutes."

"Here, honey pie." Peter held the sandwich to April's mouth.

He couldn't fathom why Lucinda acted so catty, but he wasn't going to let April think for one second that he agreed.

Tears glossed April's eyes as she shook her head. "I've had enough."

"You've only had one bite."

"Bite!" Matilda opened her little mouth wide.

"Shore." Peter gave his baby sister a bite, then took one himself. He held the sandwich back up to April's mouth. Talking around the food, he said, "See? It's yore turn now."

Matilda twisted around and bobbed her head. "Turns. Share. Good!"

April pasted on a smile and took the tiniest bite possible.

Tobias stood and looked at everyone. "I'm sorry if feathers got ruffled. Lucinda was nervous."

Peter stared up at his friend. "There's nervous, and then there's wicked mean."

"Iff'n any of mine got that fresh-mouthed, they'd be tasting a cake of lye soap." Aunt Eunice folded her arms across her chest. "A hickory switch iff'n they'd show half that much—"

Pa cut in, " 'Cept for Caleb, Tobias, yore the eldest Chance here. 'Tisn't my place to tell you what to do, but I'm more'n riled. Mayhap you oughtta take Miz Youngblood home to her folks."

Tobias left.

Pa turned to Peter. "Hit'll take three days or so for the material to get there onc't we send a telegram. Not to say that we don't 'preciate all yore hard work, but with so many of the Chances gone and you bein' there to holp with the horses and court April, we've managed to get along. I'm of a mind to send you to San Francisco with yore sis."

Johnna laughed delightedly. "Thank you, Pa! April, you could come with us!"

"O'er my dead body." Ma shook her head. "Wouldn't be

seemly, what with them courtin'. 'Sides, absence makes the heart grow fonder."

"Don't know about that," Peter said. "I'm already right fond of this here beauty. If anything, I'm afeared some other buck's gonna try to steal her away whilst I'm gone."

❧

"Have a safe trip." April passed a box to Peter. The MacPhersons needed all of their wagons, and with some of the Chances still gone, Caleb offered to have Peter and Johnna borrow one for their trip to San Francisco.

"Now you jist hang on a minute." He set the box on the porch railing. "First thangs first. Honey pie, I'm startin' to miss you, and I ain't even left yet."

"Don't you even want to know what's in the box?"

He tugged her into his arms. Dipping his head, his breath tickling her ear, Peter murmured, "You're more interestin' than anything in the whole wide world."

She shivered. *Dear Mercy, Peter's my friend. I can't have feelings for him this way.* April did her best to sound lighthearted. "You wouldn't be saying that if you knew I got up early this morning to bake you the sticky buns I've been promising."

"Yore sweeter'n any old sticky buns. Still, thankee for makin' them. I'll relish ever' last one."

"You'd better." Caleb tugged her away from Peter, and April suddenly felt very lonely. Her brother groused, "It's Wednesday. April always makes those sticky buns for us. Not today. She boxed them up and threatened if we so much as opened the lid, she'd never make them again."

"That's right." A spurt of joy filled her when Peter snatched up the box.

Johnna giggled from the wagon bench. "You Chance boys are just outta luck. Chances might always share, but Peter's a MacPherson."

Caleb poked Peter in the chest. "If you won't share, I won't either."

"You don't have anything he wants," April shot back.

As Caleb's arm wrapped around her, Peter shook his head. "Honey pie, that's where yore wrong as wrong cain be. Yore brother has you."

"You don't have to give me the whole box." Caleb smiled audaciously. "You can keep one bun for yourself."

By now, all of her brothers and cousins had lined up. "That's right," Cole said. "And once Caleb gets the box, he'll share with the rest of us."

"Now jist a minute." Johnna scowled. "I aim to have one, too!"

"I shouldn't have bothered to put them in a box," April muttered as Peter handed over the buns.

Kate, the egg basket hanging from her arm, came toward them. "So help me, if you boys are trying to steal those sticky buns from Peter, I'm not going to cook a lick of food for you for a week."

"April's cooking again," Caleb called back.

"I might be, but then again, I might not." April tilted her chin upward.

"She won't if you steal away the courting gift she's made for Peter." Kate sailed past them and into the kitchen cabin.

"Aww, man." Caleb grimaced. "Sis, are those sticky buns a courting gift?"

"What else would they be?" The jubilant look on Peter's face started April into a fit of giggles.

Matt Salter came over to see what the commotion was about. "What's going on?" He sniffed, and his eyes lit up. "What's that I smell?"

"We've got to be headin' out." Peter dared to lean down and rest his forehead against hers. "Don't you forget what I've been tellin' you."

Her heart plummeted. He'd been advising her on how to go about catching another man's interest. *I'm such a fool.* Unable to speak, she stepped back and nodded.

Caleb shoved the box into Peter's arms.

"You mean he's taking away whatever it is that smells so good?" Matt sounded outraged.

"April and I are going to go bake another batch." Kate came back out and slipped her hand into April's. "Peter, there's something in that box for your sister. Make sure she gets it."

"I'll be shore she gets one of these buns."

"That, too." Kate tugged on April's hand. "We'll end up standing here all day if I don't tear the two of you apart. Come on into the kitchen."

Once the screen door shut behind them, Kate let out a sigh. "I'm so glad you didn't ask what I put in the box. I didn't have a chance to tell you, but I wrote a little note and told Johnna we wanted her to buy some pretty things for herself. I signed it from both of us and put in a double eagle."

"Twenty dollars!" April gaped at her cousin.

Merry laughter bubbled out of Kate. "Mama left me more than that in case something came up. Now we'd better start a batch of sticky buns, or the boys are going to get ugly."

The only ugly one around here is me. April reached around and retied her apron. "May as well get busy."

≈

As April pulled the second dozen from the oven, Kate went to the porch and barely hit the huge iron triangle they used to call everyone to supper. She raced back inside. "Watch out. We've got a stampede headed our way."

The back door opened. "I ah. . .remembered how they all came in the front when you made the beef and rice." Matt stood there with his hat in his hands.

"No need to be sheepish. You're smart!" Kate nudged him

toward the table. April noticed how Kate stayed beside him.

Caleb barreled through the doorway. "Jeff Borley's here. Wants to buy another horse."

"I've never seen a man buy a horse at the kitchen table," Packard grumbled, reaching for a bun and scowling as Jeff entered the kitchen

Jeff took a sticky bun. After the first bite, he straightened up. "Feed me more of these, and you could talk me into buying both of those mares!"

"Hear that, sis?" Caleb grinned.

"So these are the sticky buns Peter MacPherson was bragging about." Jeff reached down and greedily helped himself to a second bun, even though he hadn't finished the first. "I'm going to have to come pay my respects to you, April."

"Too late," Kate said. "Peter's been coming by all summer."

"It's not too late." Jeff smacked his lips. "There's no ring on her finger."

April pretended she didn't hear him. Jeff never so much as once traded a greeting with her at church or in town. Peter's words echoed in her mind. *Don't you e'er make the mistake of thankin' your only worth is a batch of sommat you pull outta the oven.* Clearly, Jeff felt otherwise.

The kitchen grew noisy with all eight of her brothers and cousins, Matt, Kate, and Jeff. April scooted past them and onto the porch. She started turning the handle on the Daisy butter churn.

"You're industrious." Jeff's voice came from just a few feet away.

April shrugged. "We've had extra milk all summer. No use letting it go to waste."

He hitched a pantleg and perched on the porch railing. "That doesn't smell. When my mom and sis make butter, it stinks."

"I'm making sweet cream butter. My father likes it better."

Jeff hooked his thumbs into belt hoops. "Way to a man's heart is through his stomach."

"I wouldn't know. Daddy loved me long before I was old enough to cook."

"Time'll come when your father's not the one you'll stand in front of the stove for. Are you going to use the buttermilk to make biscuits for dinner?"

She shook her head. "I'm planning to make flapjacks for breakfast tomorrow." *So you can stop angling for an invitation to stay to lunch.*

Caleb came outside. "So what's it going to be, Jeff—the bay or the mustang?"

"See you around." Jeff slapped his hat on his head and walked toward the stable with her brother. April couldn't remember ever feeling so relieved to see a man saunter away.

⁂

Sleep wouldn't come. Kate blew out a resigned breath. "Are you asleep?"

"No."

Turning over and propping her chin in her hand, Kate squinted across the dark loft at April. "It must feel wonderful, having men stop by to pay their respects to you."

"Not a one has stopped by to pay his respects."

"Could have fooled me. In three days, you've had Jeff, Grayson, Horace, Enoch, and Everett come see you."

"Peter's talked about my cooking, and Jeff happened by and got a taste of my sticky buns. Men talk about animals, weather, and food. Folks didn't pay much attention to what Peter said about my cooking since the MacPhersons are famous for liking odd dishes. Once Jeff said something, they all got curious. They don't respect me. They respect my cooking. There's a world of difference."

Kate absently ran her finger along the stitch line of her quilt. "You can't be sure of that."

"Oh, I'm dead sure. Not a one discussed anything but my ability to cook and sew."

"Men think more practically."

"Which is why each of them managed to show up at mealtime." April huffed. "They wanted to taste my cooking, but none of them bothered to try to sit by me."

"Give it a chance. It takes time."

"I don't want to," April said. "They've ignored me forever, and now they're reckoning even a short, dumpy woman like me is worth considering because I'd ease his life by being a housekeeper and cook."

"You're not dumpy! You don't eat any more than the rest of us. I've seen pictures of your grandma and her mama. You're shaped just like them—like a happy little chickadee!"

April snorted. "So now I'm a bird brain. Well, I still have enough sense to send those so-called suitors packing. Enoch talked about me the same way he talks about a horse he wants to buy. I'm surprised he didn't ask to see my teeth."

After her giggles died down, Kate figured this was as good a time as any to say something. She gathered her courage. "April, I need you to do me a favor."

"What?"

"I've been keeping the boys away while your suitors come. I need you to do the same for me. My brothers won't let me have a minute alone with Matt."

April sat bolt upright and squeaked, "You've been leaving me alone with them on purpose?"

"Of course I have."

"Don't!"

"How was I to know that's what you wanted? For four years now, you've been mooning and moping over men. You've even cried over not having swains seek you out. Now that they're swarming, you're not happy getting what you wanted."

"I don't want any of them!" April flopped back down, turned on her tummy, and started sobbing into her pillow. "I've made such a mess of things!"

twelve

Kate climbed out of bed and went over to April. "You haven't made a mess of anything." She slid in next to her cousin and petted her hair.

April turned toward her. Tears continued to pour down her face as she wailed, "I've been living a lie, but now it's the truth. I don't know what to do."

"You? A lie?" Kate couldn't hide the surprise in her voice.

April nodded. "It's been a secret between Peter and me. He's pretended to like me so I could practice how to act with a suitor. Only now, I don't want any of those other men. I want Peter!"

Kate couldn't believe her ears. Ever since last year's trip to Yosemite, she'd known Peter loved her cousin. Part of her wanted to tell April so, but something kept her from doing that. Slowly, she said, "I don't know that you've been living a lie. Deep down, your heart knew what your head didn't. You and Peter have always been close."

Mournfully shaking her head, April wailed, "It's ruined now. Before he left, he told me to remember what he's taught me. He's ready to move on and find a wife. I can't stay here and watch that. I can't!"

Kate wrapped her arms around her cousin and held tight. "You're not going anywhere. We're going to pray about this."

"I've been praying. I have for years. I kept begging God to give me the right man. You know I have."

"We both have." Kate scooted closer still. "It's not easy to see God's will. I want more time alone with Matt because—well, because deep down, I think he's the one for me."

"I'd be so happy for you if he is."

Kate sighed. *Sweet April—here she is, afraid of losing Peter, and I'm telling her that I've found my man. I'm an idiot for saying anything at all, but this was the worst time I could have told her how I feel. Her heart's breaking.*

April rubbed her cheek on the pillow to wipe away her tears. "Matt fits in. It's like he's always been here. And that first night, he stood up for you even though he thought it would cost him his job. I wish Peter loved me like that."

I still think he does. The words were on the tip of Kate's tongue, but they wouldn't come out. Instead, she turned the conversation in a different direction. "Just a year ago, you and I were comforting Laurel about whether she'd ever marry Gabe. Back then, you said we had to have faith—that God wouldn't let us all be without husbands."

"He won't. He's already given Laurel Gabe, and it's looking like you and Matt are a good match. Maybe I'm supposed to be a spinster. I've been so busy telling God to give me a husband, I didn't ask if He wanted me to have one."

Aching silence filled the loft. Finally, Kate quietly admitted, "I've been doing the same thing."

Isn't that just like me, God? I'm always running full tilt at whatever catches my attention without thinking ahead. How many times have Daddy and Mama told me to stop and think? I've been so busy letting my head and heart rule me, I didn't seek Your will. I sort of figured since Matt is a good Christian, the soul part was taken care of.

April wiggled and rested her head on Kate's shoulder. "Remember what we always say when we get into fixes like this?"

"You mean before we pray?"

In unison, they whispered, "God help us all."

Kate went on, "Lord, we need Your help and direction. . . ."

&

Matt stifled a yawn. The steady cadence of pushing and pulling the two-man saw with Tanner demanded physical effort, but he let his mind wander. The middle-of-the-night explorations were catching up with him. So far, he'd inspected the entire Chance Ranch and found no evidence of a still.

Lord, these are salt-of-the-earth, God-fearing people, and it bothers me to be here under false pretenses. I'm trying to do right. Early as it is to say, I'm even feeling like You brought me here to meet Kate. She's something else. But how will she feel when I tell her I've come here pretending to be a saddle tramp?

The saw paused while both men wiped away sweat with their sleeves. Tanner raised his brows. "Wish you would have stayed back helping Cole and Paxton with the horses?"

"I can muck out stalls any day. This is a good change."

Tanner nodded and squinted in the distance. "Caleb and Tobias said they marked one more tree. We don't want to overtimber."

Matt nodded. "Someone got too rambunctious on the spread over that-a-way."

"Dorseys." Tanner wrapped his hands around the wooden saw handle. "Yep. Only good thing about that cutting was that when their barn burned, there wasn't much else to go up in flames."

"Probably saved your spread from going up." Matt grabbed his side of the saw and got back into the push-pull rhythm. One quick survey of the Dorseys' holding told him the truth. They'd cut down so much of the timber, it would be impossible to hide a still anywhere on the property.

Thaddeus Walls, even though he'd lost his family due to drunkenness, proved to be completely incapable of being any part of an illegal operation. He'd been in a drunken stupor both nights when Matt went to spy on him. The bottles littering his property showed he bought the cheapest rotgut available. Anyone owning a still or being part of the operation would save the bottles to refill or have jugs or a keg instead.

The MacPhersons still remained suspect. Matt yawned again as he recalled skulking around part of the MacPherson place the last two nights. The first time, he'd seen some activity far off toward a treeline. The second time, he'd riled a few dogs and had to leave before someone in that huge clan discovered his presence. *The best way to check them out is for me to have an excuse to be on their property.*

"Hey!" Tanner shouted.

Matt halted and looked around the tree trunk at him.

"We've gone deep enough." He grinned. "Only time I've ever seen men lose track of the work they're doing is when they've started falling in love. You've been doting on Kate. Are you thinking of her?"

"Might be." Matt shrugged. "It's none of your business, though."

"She's my sister. Of course it's my business!"

"Let's shove over this tree." Matt moved the saw and stepped to the far side. "All clear?"

"Yep." Tanner hollered, "Timber!" and the two thrust their weight against the tree. The tree groaned loudly, then the air whistled through the limbs as it began to tilt. "Got it!" Tanner and Matt scrambled backward and off to the side so they'd be out of danger if the trunk bounced.

Soon, several of the Chance men worked on the fallen tree. Some cut off limbs while others hitched the severed pieces to a team of horses and dragged them off a ways.

Pausing a moment, Packard called to no one in particular, "Our folks are going to be glad they stayed gone awhile longer."

Chuckles met that observation.

"Dunno about that!" someone on the far side of the tree shouted back. "Uncle Dan likes working his problems out with an axe."

Tobias smacked Matt on the back. "Ready to go cut down the other one?"

"Hey. Matt and I are a team." Tanner scowled at his brother.

"You *were* a team. The next tree is mine."

Matt shrugged and hiked after Tobias. Tobias picked up the saw and gave him a piercing look. "Dad'll be home in a day or so. Between now and then, I'm the head of our family. My sis might seem tough and capable, but she's got a tender heart. I don't want you breaking it."

"Kate is capable. She's smart, too. I don't believe in dallying with a woman's heart. I enjoy her company and get the notion that she could like me—but it's sorta hard to tell. You and Tanner act like a couple of watch dogs."

"We take care of our women."

"If the day comes where what's between Kate and me gets serious, you can be sure I'll take care of her."

"That's what worries me—you said *if.* You're not sure how you feel. She's already getting her heart set on you. You being underfoot all of the time makes it easy for her to plan out a future."

"I don't know what my future holds. I have to leave it in God's hands. If He gives me Kate as my wife, I'd be a very blessed man."

"Gals are just like birds. Doesn't matter how fancy or drab they are, they still wanna nest. It's in their nature."

"If you're trying to compare Lucinda to Kate, don't." Matt stared at Tobias. "I don't know anything more about Lucinda than what I saw at the picnic. I am positive, however, Kate wouldn't ever cut down another person—not even on her worst day."

Tobias winced. "I didn't mean to make a comparison, but I can see how you thought I did. I've never seen Lucinda act like that."

That admission hadn't come easy. Matt chose to move on. "Kate tried to hide her hands from me. I don't know where she got the ridiculous notion that dabs of stain would matter to a man. She's beautiful, inside and out."

They came to the other tree Caleb had marked. Just as they set the saw against the tree, the dinner triangle jangled.

Tobias's brow wrinkled. "It can't be lunch."

The jangling didn't stop. "Something's wrong!"

thirteen

Matt and Tobias simultaneously let go of the two-handled saw and ran for their horses. The other men dropped their axes and joined them. Those whose horses were hitched to branches hurried to release them, but Matt didn't wait. He vaulted onto his mount and raced toward the cabins.

"Don't see any smoke!" Packard shouted.

Kate. Matt urged his horse on.

"Cole better not have tried to break that stallion." Distress and anger tainted Tobias's voice. "I shouldn't have left him there. I knew he was tempted."

"Ringing stopped." Packard rode on Matt's other side. "Someone's hurt. Kate and April must be busy trying to help."

Lord, I don't want anyone harmed, but please—especially not Kate.

Their horses skidded to an abrupt halt in the barnyard. Relief flooded Matt when he spied Kate standing on the porch clutching the striker that belonged to the triangle.

The men bolted from their saddles. "Where?" Caleb demanded at the same time Tobias yelled, "Who?"

"Everyone is okay!" Kate called back.

April stood by her side and yelled, "Nothing's wrong!"

"Then what did you think you were doing?" Caleb bellowed as he started toward her.

Matt jumped in front of him. He wasn't sure whether to fight Caleb or shake Kate until her teeth rattled. She'd given him a fright.

Lucinda pushed between the Chance girls and stepped

forward. Her lower lip poked out in a pout, she said, "That's what I asked them, too."

"Kate?" Matt's tone demanded an explanation. Relief continued to pour through him at the sight of her.

"Forget it." Cole strode over from the stables. "Lucinda came over and couldn't find anyone."

"So I rang the triangle." Lucinda didn't seem apologetic at all. "At least that made folks show up."

The rest of the men tore around the corner and came to a dead halt. "Everything's all right!" Tobias yelled.

"Then who set out the alarm?"

"Since you men are here," April said, "we may as well put lunch on the table."

"Go ahead and wash up." Kate turned toward the door. "I'll get the dishes."

Matt wasn't going to let her out of his sight until he reassured himself that she was all right. He rushed to open the door for her. "Sure everything's okay?" he asked quietly.

Her gaze darted over to Lucinda. Tobias stood close to her and was speaking in a hushed, forceful tone. Kate looked back up at Matt. "I guess the important thing is that no one's hurt."

Several more horses thundered into the yard. Matt hadn't seen the riders before, but he knew in an instant they were Kate's father and uncles. "What's wrong?"

"Nothing's wrong, Dad." Tobias let out a beleaguered sigh. "It's all a misunderstanding. Welcome home."

A tall man with silver at his temples hopped off his horse straight onto the porch. "Are you okay, Katie Louise?"

"I'm fine, Daddy." She stood on tiptoe and kissed his cheek.

"Good." He turned and glowered at Matt. "Who are you, and why are you holding my daughter's hand?"

Just then, a bunch of MacPhersons arrived, demanding to

know what the emergency was. Matt ignored them. He stuck out his hand. "I'm Matthew Salter, sir."

"Our new hired hand, Daddy. He's a hard worker."

Matt didn't for an instant mistake the possessive spark in Kate's father's eyes. Something even more possessive flared inside him. "As for holding your daughter's hand, well, I've never seen a more lovely one."

"It's got stain on it."

Matt shook his head. "Better look again. Those are beauty marks."

❧

April wound her arms around Mama. "I'm so glad you're home!"

"It's good to be home."

"Daniel, put me down," Aunt Lovejoy said. When he refused, she reached over and cupped April's cheek. "April-mine, we went past the MacPhersons'. My sister tole me about you and Peter. Hit's about time. Two of you b'long to one another."

Guilt churned inside, and April blinked back tears.

"Why are you crying, honey?" Mama asked.

"They're happy tears," Kate said. "But she misses Peter. He and Johnna went to San Francisco."

Uncle Obie snorted. "April ain't the onliest one missin' that son of mine. He's a hard worker."

Uncle Titus folded his arms across his chest. "With all of us back, we'll do just fine. I understand our new hand, Salter, isn't a stranger to work. We'll loan him to you."

Kate gasped, "Daddy!"

"I don't mind, Kate." The corner of Matt's mouth kicked upward. "After all, you've told me on more than one occasion that Chances share."

"Won't be for long." Obie combed his fingers through his

beard. "I reckon Peter and Johnna'll be home in two more days."

Mama gave April a tender smile. "Quicker than that if he's missing April half as much as she's missing him."

"Don't mean to rush you folks, but I need to tuck Lovejoy into bed."

"I'll do that!" April chased after Uncle Daniel. "You go on ahead and eat lunch. I'd love to visit with her and hear what she liked best in Yosemite."

"That's a grand plan." Lovejoy patted Daniel. "You jist tole me how hungry you are." April rushed forward to open the door to their cabin and turn down their sheets. Uncle Dan gave his wife a kiss and gently settled her on the bed. "Stop frettin', Dan'l. Get on out thar and eat hearty."

For the past week, Kate and April had been putting a fresh pitcher of water in all of the cabins just in case their family got home. Now she poured water into the basin and dampened a washcloth. All at once, doubts assailed her. *I can't believe I volunteered to come in here. I was afraid Mama would figure out something's wrong, but Aunt Lovejoy knows me just as well.*

Daniel left, and April pasted on a smile as she turned around.

Aunt Lovejoy let out a sigh. "Darlin', I don't mean you no offense, but I'm plumb wore out. All I want is to lie down and take a nap like I'm ninety years old."

"The day we came home, I was at least ninety. You have to be ninety-nine." She gently washed her aunt's face and hands.

"Ahhh. Nothin' feels finer than comin' clean."

It took no time at all to slip her aunt out of her dusty clothes and into a fresh nightgown. April tucked her into bed and brushed a kiss on her pain-etched face. "Welcome home."

"It's good to be home. Onliest thang that don't feel complete is my Polly and baby Ginny Mae aren't here."

As soon as Lovejoy drifted off to sleep, April walked the long way around to the stable so she could avoid everyone. She saddled up her mustang and rode to town. Lovejoy deserved to see Polly and her grandbaby. Besides, April had to think.

Lord, I don't know what to do. It's all such a mess. I don't feel good about asking You to fix this when it's my fault. The people I care about the most are going to be disappointed in me. I've used Peter to reach my selfish goals, and I've misled everyone else. I know I have to pay the consequences, Father, but could You please work things out so no one else does?

When she reached town, April headed straight for the doctor's office. Old Mrs. Greene hobbled out of Eric's office and smiled at her. "Doc Walcott's in. You here to see him or visit Polly and that cute little baby of theirs?"

"I'm hoping they're not busy. Everyone got home from Yosemite, and Lovejoy wants to see them."

"I heard that!" Polly sang out.

April laughed and let herself in. Polly enveloped her in a hug.

"Eric's seeing a patient; then he needs to go pay a visit on the pastor's kids. Ginny Mae finally got down for her nap. I can pack for us, and we'll come spend the night."

"Need some help?"

Polly's eyes lit with humor. "Actually, what we really need are some sourballs. Eric's out, and he always gives his pediatric patients a sourball. Would you mind running over to White's and grabbing them?"

"I don't mind at all."

Mrs. White was busy measuring out yardage for Mrs. Dorsey, so April took the lid off the big jar of sourballs and started filling a quart jar when the bell over the door rang.

"April!" Peter's voice rang through the mercantile. "What're you doin' here?"

"Getting sourballs," Mrs. Dorsey said.

April wanted to crawl into the corner and hide. Everyone in the place was going to think she was buying sweets for herself.

Peter hadn't stopped in the doorway. He strode straight to her. "Put 'em down, honey pie. I aim to claim a hug."

"Here?"

Mrs. White bustled over. "Young love. It's so sweet. April, hand me that little jar. I'll fill it for Doc. Peter's looking impatient, and I don't want these candies to roll all over the floor."

Being in his arms felt right. April allowed herself a second to relish his closeness one last time before she ended things and set him free to find a girl he could love.

"Missed me?"

She nodded.

The bell rang again. Johnna said, "Peter, you said you were jist gonna pick up the mail. What's—oh. Hi, April! I want to hurry home so I cain still see Trevor afore it goes dark."

"We ain't hurrying anywhere with those big crates full of material Gabe sent."

April tried to sound casual. "Johnna, you're welcome to borrow my horse. I'm sure Peter can get me home."

"Oh, thankee!" Johnna wheeled around, but the door no more than shut when it opened and jangled the bell again. "Where's yore horse?"

"In front of Eric and Polly's."

Peter chuckled. "Well that proves that love is blind. Eric and Polly are right across the street!"

They collected the mail, delivered the sourballs, then Peter curled his hands around her waist and lifted her into the buckboard. He looked her in the eyes. "I'm glad you sent my sister on ahead. I sorely need to talk with you."

April felt sure her heart had dropped right out of her chest and Peter had run it over with the buckboard. It took every bit of her courage to stay on the seat beside him. As soon as they'd gotten out of town, she blurted out, "Everyone's home."

"Is that a fact?"

"Yes. Peter, you're right we need to talk. I've gotten us into a horrible mess."

fourteen

"Horrible mess?" April's words cut deeply. Peter had decided he had to come clean and confess his love to her.

"I've prayed for years for the man God intended to be my husband. Instead of waiting patiently for God to prepare me, I roped you into getting me ready. I should have known better and trusted in His timing. Instead, now everyone thinks we're in love. It's the very first thing Mama and Aunt Lovejoy said to me."

"Afore you go blaming yoreself any further, you need to recollect 'twas my idea to come calling and teach you thangs you needed to know."

"Only after I cried all over your shirt."

"I ain't never once felt anything but honored to spend time with you. I've tole you afore, I'm here to share yore joys and sorrows."

"I was afraid you were going to do that—be all honorable."

He gave her an exasperated look. "Most gals would be afeared a buck wouldn't be honorable."

"I'll have to confess to our families. It's my fault."

The horses knew the way home, so he focused his attention fully on her. "Are you miserable o'er having to swaller yore pride and tell them, or are you upset on account of how you might feel deep down inside?"

Pain flashed across her face. "Don't ask me that!"

He cupped her face between his hands. "I gotta ask. Time's come for truth, April. You ain't been o'er my spread on account of havin' so much extry to do back home with so many gone.

I cleared a spot, and we've all been spending time putting up a cabin. That cabin is for me and my true love."

She closed her eyes and swallowed hard. In a tight voice, she whispered, "I hope she makes you happy."

"Yore the one who makes me happy."

Tears seeped out as she scrunched her eyes even tighter. "You're being noble. I was afraid of this."

"Noble?" He snorted. "Gal, I been crazy in love with you for over a year now. I been a-waitin' for you to fall in love with me. All this business 'bout me holpin' you catch a man was jist an excuse for me to be 'round you more."

Her eyes opened, but he couldn't interpret what she was thinking. "The whole time I've been gone, I near worried myself sick, thankin' on how other bucks would come a-callin'."

Her eyes dilated.

"They have!"

He heaved a deep breath and let go of her face, only to grab both of her hands. "I knew onc't they realized how special you are, I'd have to wrastle for your love. But I ain't a-gonna let you go. 'Member what I tole you afore I left?"

"You told me to remember everything you'd said." Her voice went ragged. "How to build a man up, to make him feel special—"

"No, no! Not that. I meant about how you got a heart full of tenderness and sweet words trip off yore tongue. Not to let a man jist look at you as the gal who makes tasty food. Yore value is far above rubies."

Not sure she was convinced, Peter halted the wagon and looked around. He hopped down, pulled April down, and didn't turn loose of her. She waited a second, then tilted her head up to give him a startled look. He yanked her into a hug. "I ain't a-turnin' loose of you."

"You stopped in the middle of the road to give me a hug?"

"Ain't no better reason." He grinned.

For an instant, one of her beautiful smiles burst through, but it dimmed just as quickly. "I don't suppose you noticed there's less of me. I've been trying—"

He pressed his fingers over her lips. "Shhh." He looked around and ordered, "Go yonder to that shady spot. I'll be there in a jiffy."

He rummaged in the boxes and crates, then went over to kneel by April's side. Carefully setting two candles on a flat rock, he looked at her. He lit the short, round pillar first, then the tall, narrow taper. Sitting back on his heels, he whispered a prayer. "Tell me, honey pie. Which candle gives the most light?"

"It doesn't make any difference."

" 'Zactly. God don't make His children all alike. Some folks are tall and skinny like that taper; others are stocky. Our Creator sets fire to our souls, and we're to be His light. How could you thank I'd care 'bout something that don't matter one whit?"

April's gaze dropped from his, back to the candles. "Lucinda is right. Gluttony is a sin."

"That's 'tween you and God. Ain't nobody else's business to judge."

"But they do."

"Most sins are hidden in the heart. Folks cain foster greed, lust, envy, or wrath in secret or jist show that side of their character to one other person. Sloth—well, folks don't show that flaw in public. Gluttony's the onliest one that shows on the outside.

"Gluttony is eatin' and drinkin' to excess. That bein' said, I cain't honestly say I've e'er seen you eat more'n anybody else. Kate's remarked on that, too. My uncle Mike—well, he's downright runty and scrawny compared to my pa or my uncle Hezzie."

A smile flickered across her face.

Heartened by that fleeting smile, Peter winked. "Don't you niver tell him I said so. But 'tis the truth, and we both know it's so. Anyhow, Uncle Mike—I cain't recollect a single meal where he didn't eat as much or more'n his brothers. Anybody jist a-lookin' at him might assume he eats less, but appearances and actuality—well, they're worlds apart. Could be, God fashioned you to be short and round to begin with. Whether you added on a little more, only you and He know."

He took her hand in his. "Not a one of us is perfect. God holps us, works with us to be more like Him. You and me—we both yearn to be what God wants us to be. We gotta harken to His voice and follow His will. Philippians says, 'Being confident of this very thing, that he which hath begun a good work in you will perform it until the day of Jesus Christ.' We cain be confident He'll lead us aright."

"That's talking about our relationship with Him. What about other people?"

"He don't compare us to anybody. He loves us jist 'cuz we're His. We get ourselves into trouble when we compare. Iff'n a thin person starts makin' comparisons, then Lucifer has a high old time lettin' pride seep in. Lucinda sat there, preening and actin' all superior when she decided to judge you. 'Twas a stingy heart she showed that day, but you cain't let yoreself believe that ever'body who's lanky feels the way she does."

She twitched him a smile. "That's true."

He paused and tucked a wisp of hair back behind her ear.

"April, iff'n you compare yoreself to a gal who cinches herself 'til she's got a fourteen-inch waist, yore takin' yore eyes off God. Lets the devil have a chance to make you feel defeated."

She nodded slowly. "I do feel beaten down."

"That saddens me no end. April, yore the most beautiful gal I've e'er seen. I reckon I could tell you how yore fine brown hair sparkles in the sunshine and when 'tis silvered with age I'll love you all the more, but that ain't what you need to know most."

She chewed on her lower lip.

Lord, holp me here. I don't wanna be vulgar. Peter's gaze swept across her and back to her eyes. "In the Bible, in the Song of Solomon, when that feller tells his gal how he feels—I feel that way 'bout you. Yore generous—in heart and of body. I cain't holp thanking how much a man would be blessed to come home each night to you. Yore body was made to cuddle a man and cradle babes. Nothin' would please me more than to be that man."

Pink tinted her cheeks, and her eyes widened—but she didn't look away from him.

He reached over and pinched out the flame on the taper and lifted the pillar. "You already let yore light shine, April. My heart warms by it's glow. I'm askin' you to become my wife."

"Oh, Peter. I love you. Nothing would make me happier."

ta.

An almost sickening sweetness hovered in the air. Matt inhaled and looked around. *If the moonshiner is using sweet mash instead of sour mash, it might smell like this. But the wind's blowing from over by the MacPhersons' cabins. I've managed a glimpse inside all of them, and none holds a still.*

He'd been at the MacPherson spread for a full week and a half. They might be as simple and straightforward as they seemed, but with so many of them going different ways, he hadn't been able to determine whether they managed to have a few members slip off and run a still. They sort of rotated through certain chores, but Matt couldn't see a pattern emerge.

"Bet you never thought you'd be lumberjackin' instead of cowboyin'," Peter teased.

Together, they heaved another log onto the pile. "It's for a good cause."

"I want this cabin to look jist like the one April's leavin'. The loft'll give us plenty of room for young'uns."

"Why don't you all just halt everything and spend a day to erect it?"

Yanking a splinter from his palm Peter shrugged. "We got too many thangs happenin' already. Harvest hits the same time the women are cannin', and the younger ones gotta get fixed up for school. Add two weddings to that."

A bell clanged. "Lunch." Peter dusted some tree bark from his shirt.

"I'm so hungry, I could eat just about anything." Matt chuckled at the look Peter shot at him. "The 'possum pie, porcupine stew and dumplings, and rabbit were all excellent." He tactfully left out fried lizard.

"This time of year, we always give the boys the job of wrastlin' up meat. Don't normally eat such a variety in the space of a week; but with everyone busy, it lets them shoulder a responsibility."

"They're all good kids. I get a kick out of how good they are with those slingshots."

"Slingshot ain't no match for a badger. We're all grateful you was out takin' a hike last night. Octavius and Reggie woulda gotten catawamptuously chewed up iff'n you hadn't been thar. Hey! Lookie!" He started jogging.

Matt kept pace. The Chance women and young children had come to call. *I hope Kate came.*

Peter swept April up and spun her around in a circle before her down. Matt spied Kate sitting off to the side, He beelined for her. "Hi."

"Matt!" She looked up from her work. Delight danced across her features. "How are you doing over here?"

"Fine. I've whittled some clothespins. Make sure I give them to you. What're you doing?"

"Shining up a few pairs of shoes."

A little girl jumped from one bare foot to the other. "Kate's gonna turn mine red!"

Matt rested his hands on his knees and bent over so he could look into her eyes. "Won't you be a sight in pretty red shoes!"

When she nodded, the little girl's braids jumped from behind her shoulders to the front and back again. "I'll be bee-you-tea-ful!"

Kate set aside the pair of shoes she'd repaired. "Okay, Birdie. Bring me yours now."

Matt chuckled as the child hopped away. "Her name sure fits!"

Kate shot him a conspiratorial look and patted the space beside her. Glad of the invitation, he sat down. In a low tone, she said, "Her real name is Birdella. Eunice and Hezzie saddle their children with odd names."

Matt poked his tongue into the pocket of his cheek, thought a second, then said, "So they weren't kidding when they called one of the little fellows 'Lastun'?"

"That's really his name. Eunice was wrong, though. She had Elvera after him."

"I'm still trying to sort out who's who."

"And who's whose?"

"Yep. There's an army of kids here."

She dusted tiny slivers of leather from her apron. "It'll take time, but you'll manage."

"Is that your way of saying Chance Ranch doesn't need me anymore?"

Before she could reply, two women walked up. "Matthew Salter," Tempy MacPherson said, "words cain't say how grateful I am that you rescued Octavius—"

"And my Register—" Eunice added.

"Yestereve. Badgers are fearsome fighters."

Eunice shoved a bowl into his hands. "But they make a fine stew! Cain't thankee 'nuff and wanna honor you by givin' you the first bowl."

fifteen

"Thank you, ladies," Matt said. "I'm just glad the boys are okay. You know, I've never eaten badger."

"Neither have I." Kate's eyes sparkled with mischief.

"My mother would spin in her grave if I ate before a lady, Miss Kate." Matt slid the bowl to her before she could respond.

"Ain't it nice to see a man with such fine manners?" Eunice patted him on the shoulder. "Don't you worry none. I'll bring another for you now."

"Wait!" Kate used her free hand to grab Tempy. "Aunt Tempy, everyone knows how thick and meaty your stews are. One badger can't have made enough stew for all of us. Since Mama brought over beef stew, why don't we just let Mr. Salter have this? I'll have the other."

"I wouldn't want any of you feeling I didn't appreciate good cooking. Why don't I come over and get a bowl of the beef stew, then Kate and I can switch halfway through our bowls?" Matt nodded his head once to indicate it was a done deal.

"Now ain't they the most thoughtful young'uns?" Eunice beamed at them. "Nothin' like that uppity Lucin—"

"We wouldn't want to gossip," Tempy interrupted.

Eunice gave her sister-in-law a confused look. "Hit ain't gossipin' in the least. We was all thar and saw for ourselves—"

"I guess," Kate said, "it just goes to show how blessed we are to have friends and family who try to find the best in others."

"Yore right. I oughtta be ashamed of myself, standing here

131

a-ditherin' whilst Mr. Salter's powerful hungry and wantin' his lunch."

"Why don't the both of you come sit at the table?"

Kate's laughter floated on the breeze. "If I do, you'll never pry me free. After the vat of marmalade you've made and been jarring all morning, I'll either stick to the bench from the sugar or stay there because I can't resist tasting it."

"Best you stay put. Hey! Homer, don't you dare show up to the table with that much grime on you!" Tempy scurried toward one of her many children.

Matt rose and accompanied Eunice to the tables. "Not counting weddings or church picnics, other than the Mac-Phersons and the Chances, the only time I've ever seen so many people gathered along tables like this was at an orphanage."

Kate's mother jerked around and stared at him. "Did you grow up in an orphanage?"

"No, ma'am, I didn't. While I was in San Francisco, I—" He caught himself before he admitted having to take an abandoned child to the orphanage. He cleared his throat. "I dropped a little something off."

"I hope the children were all happy and well cared for."

"It sure looked that way to me, ma'am. The children had plenty of good food to eat. The girls even wore ribbons in their hair. They weren't expecting anyone to drop by, so it wasn't as if someone put on a show. I was told a wealthy benefactor provides funds to keep the place operating."

"Here you go, Mr. Salter." Eunice shoved a hot bowl into his hands. "Grab yoreself a spoon and be shore you get a taste of the badger stew, too."

"Thank you, ma'am." He strode back to Kate. "I must have missed when someone asked the blessing."

"Uncle Obie did."

Matt sat down, bowed his head for a quick prayer since he'd not heard Obie's, then said, "Did my ears deceive me, or did Eunice call her son Register?"

Kate grinned. "We call him Reggie. Vinnie and Benny are girls—their nicknames are acts of mercy. No little girl ought ever be called Vinetta or Benefit."

"I agree." He waved his spoon at her bowl. "So how does it taste?"

"I was waiting for you."

"Don't let me hold you up."

Stirring the stew with her spoon, Kate said, "We have an agreement, right? We'll trade bowls?"

"Fair's fair." He took a bite of the beef stew. "Then again, this is awfully tasty. I might not want to give it up."

Kate muttered under her breath, "Here goes nothing," and lifted her spoon. As soon as she swallowed the first bite, she gave his bowl a sideways glance.

"We don't swap until halfway." He dipped his spoon and brought up another big bite. "Your mama sure makes a flavorful stew."

He ate faster than she. Matt figured it was because Kate wasn't fond of how badger tasted. He didn't much blame her, either. In a low tone, he said, "You don't have to eat all of your half."

"I will." Resolve vibrated in her low tone.

"I appreciate a woman who sticks to her word." He cocked his head to the side and surveyed two rows of shoes all lined up in the dirt about a yard away. "Some of those shoes look pretty battered."

"Kids are hard on shoes. Simple polishing and new laces will perk most of those. Since Birdie is getting Octavius's hand-me-downs, I'll die them red so they take on a girlish look."

"That's clever of you. Is that why the pair on the end are sporting yellow leather bows?"

"Yes. The next pair to the right will be Meldona's." He raised his browns, and she nodded. "Yes, she's Eunice and Hezzie's. Melly's shoes have been passed down twice—but both times, they were girls'. I'll put some pretty new buttons on them once I banish the scuffs. They'll see her through Christmas."

"Your talent serves both clans exceedingly well."

"Your boots look like they could use a little help."

Matt lifted his empty spoon and shook it at her. "No buttons or bows for me."

Her laughter stopped abruptly when he tried to take the badger stew. "I'll finish this, Matt. You said the beef is tasty. Go ahead and enjoy it."

"Nope. I honor my word." He switched bowls, looked down at the chunks of badger meat, and consoled himself with the fact that he didn't have to eat a whole bowl all on his own. Kate watched him avidly as he lifted the spoon to his mouth.

"This is wonderful!"

"I was just as surprised as you are." She looked down at the bowl she now held. "I love my mother's stew. I didn't think anything could compare."

"So now you can have two favorites."

"I don't mean to gossip, Matt, but I think you should know something. Tobias isn't courting Lucinda anymore."

He swallowed his bite. "Appreciate knowing that so I don't go putting my foot in my mouth. Your brother's a steady man, so a big change like that had to come after a lot of soul searching."

"I'd be lying to say I'm sad, but it's hard to see him hurting." She ate a little. "On the other hand, Caleb's wife, Greta, is home again. Her sister had twins, so she was over helping out.

You might not recognize Caleb—he's found his smile again."

"I don't mean to boast, but I'm pretty good with remembering names and faces."

Kate's eyes sparkled. "But I'm telling you, Caleb's face looks entirely different. It's amazing what a smile can do."

It sure is. Your smile makes you glow. Matt tore his gaze from her. "I'll take your word for it. Seeing a new woman sitting among the Chances in the church pew will help me figure out which man is Caleb."

"Not for certain. I don't think you've met my cousin Polly. Her husband is the doctor—they live in town. Last Saturday, some men got rambunctious at the Nugget and had a gunfight. She and Eric missed church because they were still in surgery."

He whistled softly. "Either someone got hit bad, or it must've involved quite a few men."

"There's talk about the town needing to hire a sheriff. Until recently, Reliable was small enough and quiet most of the time." She let out a sigh. "I rather doubt it will happen. Folks have talked about needing someone to come reopen the boardinghouse, too. Neither has ever materialized."

Boardinghouse. His promise to drop a line to Miss Jenny flashed through Matt's mind. Later that evening, he wrote her a short note that said he was keeping busy. *Fact is, Miss Jenny, I'm seeing all those stars you knew I'd been missing. . . .* It was the truth. He'd been investigating the area during the night. *I've been eating well and met some good, God-fearing people.* He wished her God's blessings and signed the bottom, then stuffed the paper into an envelope.

Then next morning, he rode to worship along with the MacPherson men. The women and smaller children filled three buckboards. As they pulled into the churchyard, April called from the wagon she was driving, "We didn't plan a picnic, but it's a beautiful day. Are you folks interested?"

Lois looked at her husband, then nodded. "Johnna an' me—we were fixin' to look through the feedsacks and decide on what to use for the next quilt. Y'all cain come and holp. Delilah, yore always good at choosing colors that look fine together."

"That shouldn't be hard," a woman said from the church steps. "You MacPhersons always have yellow ones!"

"Reba White, 'tis mostly the sugar sacks that're yeller." Lois laughed. "Cain't manage to get the man at the feed and lumber to keep a supply of yeller feedsacks."

A man nearby let out a booming laugh. "Lois, I keep telling you, God makes all your leghorn chicks yellow, so the color of the sack doesn't matter!"

Lois pulled Matilda down from the wagon. "Bill, yore always glad to get my eggs and eat my chicken salad. Why cain't you humor me and bring in yeller sacks?"

"Because the rest of us have wives who want other colors!"

"I cain't be shore who said that, but I'll hold charity in my heart for you. Everyone as wants, come on o'er today for a picnic. 'Twould be a pity to waste a fine day like this."

"I already have a roast in the oven at home," one lady said. "Why don't we make it tomorrow? It'll let us ladies quilt!"

April's father clapped his hands. "I'll go tomorrow on one condition."

"What's that?" Pastor Abe asked.

"We men help finish the cabin Peter is building. I'd like to announce that my daughter, April, accepted his proposal. Chance Ranch will be roasting a steer, so bring your appetites along with your tools!"

The Youngbloods stood over by their buggy. Lucinda's father rumbled, "Tomorrow's a workday. I'm not stopping everything just to be fed beef. I've got plenty of my own."

"Guess he's sore angered at Tobias Chance," Johnna whispered from behind Matt. "Tobias told Lucinda they'd come to a partin' of the ways. I s'pose her daddy's got call to be a mite hot under the collar. Pa would splavocate if Trevor did that to me."

"Weren't no promise nor proposal," Tempy murmured. " 'Twas wise, Tobias calling a halt to the courtship soon as he realized 'twouldn't work out."

Looking remarkably unperturbed, Gideon Chance nodded at Lucinda's father. "It's short notice, and it's a busy time. No one's under any obligation."

"Jist you watch," Eunice said in a hushed tone. "Folks're gonna come through. Makes me glad I come out to Reliable to be Hezzie's bride. People pitch in."

"You all stopped everything when my barn burnt down to help me get back on my feet." Dorsey squared his shoulders. "It's not about what we get fed. It's about helping a neighbor."

Soon pledges of help and promises to bring food filled the churchyard. Mrs. White and Bill decided since everyone was going to be at the cabin raising, they might as well close the mercantile and feedstore.

Pastor Abe stood on the church steps. "Folks, the sermon today was entitled 'Who is My Neighbor?' I could say plenty, but you've demonstrated the heart of the concept here and now. The sanctuary windows are open, but it's far cooler out here. Why don't we gather on the lawn and have a time of prayer and worship?"

While people moved their rigs and horses to free up shady spots, Matt noticed two of the MacPhersons slip away. So did two Chance man—Daniel, who was married to Tempy MacPherson's sister, and Kate's father.

Lord, I want to stay and worship You. This time is precious, holy. I don't want to believe that these men could be guilty—especially

*not Kate's father. It would break her heart. I can't reconcile the
Christian values they've instilled in their children or the character
they've displayed with the possibility that they may be making
moonshine. But it's so suspicious that these men are slinking away. I
ought to follow them.*

"You won't need to move yore horse," Peter said. "What say
the both of us go into the church and bring out a bench or two?
Sitting on the ground'll be too hard on some of our elders."

"I didn't see benches in there—just pews."

"We keep one in each of the coatrooms." Peter started to
stride away. "Follow me."

*I'm stepping out in faith, Lord. My mind tells me to trail the
others, but my heart tells me to follow Peter.*

When they exited the church, Peter paused a moment.
"Now ain't that a sight to fill yore heart?"

Kate and April sat on either side of their frail Aunt Lovejoy.
Little children from the congregation had flocked over and sat
pressed close together. Their sweet high voices hovered in the
air as they sang the hymn, "Who Is Thy Neighbor?"

As they sang, a few quilts appeared—probably from wagon
beds. The women of the congregation spread them out until
the grass looked like a giant patchwork quilt. Men came back
from moving their rigs and joined their wives.

Pastor Abe motioned to Peter and Matt. "Good, good.
Why don't you young men bring one of those up front here?"

"I thought we'd put them off to the side or in back for the
elders," Matt said to Peter.

"Go on ahead and do that. I'll tote this one up by the
parson. Jist you wait and see. We're in for a treat."

Matt carried the bench over near Kate. Of everyone in the
congregation, her aunt looked the most frail. He went down
on one knee behind her. "Ma'am, I'd be honored to help you
up and onto that bench."

Kate's eyes sparkled with gratitude. "How nice!"

"You must be that Salter buck."

"Yes, ma'am, I am."

"I'd 'preciate the holp, but I'd take it kindly iff'n you'd get me up t'other bench instead."

Matt gently gathered her in his arms and lifted. He no more than took two steps before April's father stopped him. "I'll take her."

Lovejoy patted Matt's chest and whispered, "Don't you be takin' that as a slight to yore strength. Gideon's a-tryin' to give you a fair excuse to slide into my spot and sit yourself down aside Kate."

"That wasn't my intent," Gideon rumbled.

"Good thang you Chance boys are strong and handsome. At times yore a tad dense." Lovejoy reached over and wound her arms around her brother-in-law as Matt slid her into his arms. "Thankee, Mr. Salter, for heftin' me up. I'd a-been stuck thar like a tip-turned turtle."

"We couldn't have that," Matt whispered. "One of the MacPhersons might make soup out of you!"

Gideon Chance chuckled.

Lovejoy grinned. "If that ain't a fact, I'm a 'possum."

Matt shot back, "Eunice and Lois make a tasty 'possum pie."

April's father threw back his head and let out a belly laugh. He laughed the whole way up to the front and while he seated Lovejoy on the bench.

Matt sat down beside Kate. She turned to him. "What's so funny?"

"Not a thing." He lifted a pair of kids, straightened out his legs, then plopped them back down. Two more kids popped up and promptly sat across his shins.

Kate took in the sight. "You're not going anywhere for a while."

Matt looked at how a little tyke climbed into Kate's lap, squirmed into a comfortable position, and started sucking his thumb. "Neither are you. I wouldn't change things one bit."

Discordant twangs and pings made Matt look up. Tempy and Johnna each held a mandolin, Lovejoy had a dulcimer, Titus Chance was tuning his guitar, and Peter drew his bow across a fiddle. A quick glance around showed the MacPhersons and Chances who'd left earlier were all back. Relief flooded Matt. He settled in for a time of worship.

"Since Pastor wanted today to be about neighbors, why don't we do the one. . .you know. . . ." Mrs. White began to sing, *"Ye neighbors, and friends of Jesus, draw near."*

Members of the congregation joined in, and as soon as that hymn ended, the pastor stood and prayed. He scanned the people seated across the lawn. "The Spirit is here among us. Let's continue to worship in word and song. If anyone wants to give a word of praise or thanksgiving, needs prayer, or wants to request a hymn, please feel free."

Lovejoy looked at Tempy. Matt couldn't hear what she said, but they both started to play "O Praise Our God Today."

April and Kate immediately raised their voices, *"His constant mercy bless."* At the end of the hymn, Kate said, "That's Aunt Tempy's favorite."

Peter started to speak. His gaze rested on April. "A man cain't be blessed more'n God givin' him a woman whose value is far 'bove rubies. Y'all heard April's to be my wife, and my heart near bursts with love for her and for a Lord who brung her to me. 'Tis hard to sing and play a fiddle at the same time, but 'Now Thank We All Our God,' shore suits me today."

After a few testimonies, prayers, and hymns, the pastor rose again. "Almighty Father, we thank Thee for being with us always—not just on Sunday mornings, but each hour of every day of the week. How wonderful it is to be surrounded by a great church family that practices Thy commandment to love our neighbors! Bless and keep us all in the center of Thy will. Amen."

During the worship, little Matilda had crawled into April's lap. She had fallen asleep, as had the boy sitting on Kate's lap. Parents came over and claimed the children perched on Matt's legs, but he wasn't in a hurry to get up. He reached over and traced the whorls of curls on the little boy's head.

Stooping in front of April, Peter scooped up his baby sister. He rose, then extended a hand to help April rise. Tobias bumped past them and pulled what had to be the youngest Chance kid from the blanket. "Come on, Perry." He tilted him upside down and shook him just for fun.

Kate laughed. Abruptly, her laughter stopped and she went tense.

Matt followed her gaze and shot to his feet.

sixteen

Matt took a few steps forward and stuck out his hand. "Youngblood. Matt Salter. It's good to see your wife's feeling better. Sorry she took sick last Sunday."

Tobias turned Perry right side up and shoved him behind his back.

Mr. Youngblood's eyes narrowed; then he bobbed his head as he shook Matt's hand. "Yes, she was better once I got her in out of the sun."

Kate patted her little cousin and ordered, "Off to the wagon." *This isn't the place or time, Lord. Please don't let things get ugly.* She wanted to nudge Tobias to silently urge him to make a tactful getaway. Matt had been clever enough to stall for him, but Tobias didn't budge.

Mr. Youngblood turned to Peter. "I was harsh earlier. My wife and I wish you every happiness. I'll send a man or two over tomorrow to help."

Peter shook his hand. "Thankee, sir."

Mr. Youngblood strode off.

April wilted into Peter's side, and Tobias's features eased.

"You're the only Chance gal who isn't spoken for," Mr. Greene said as he claimed his little son.

Heat filled Kate's cheeks. Mr. Greene was a fine blacksmith, but he had no talent for exercising tact. *He's just saying aloud what everyone else is thinking.*

Tobias slapped Greene on the back. "Kate's like Aunt Lovejoy. Children adore her. Bet it won't take long before someone snaps her up."

Kate started to get up. Tobias and Matt both reached to help her at the same time. She accepted both hands and rose. "Thank you, gentlemen."

"Peter."

Peter and April turned to face Tobias.

In a muted voice, he said, "We'll still have a picnic at your place today. Give us time to go home and change into work clothes. You'll need more logs for the cabin raising tomorrow, and the ox is in the ditch."

"I'd appreciate that."

Matt nodded his head sagely, but he couldn't suppress his grin. "That has to be the first time I've heard someone refer to the scripture that allows hard work on the Lord's Day. Most men quote how it's supposed to be a day of rest."

"Reckon I've only heard it onc't or twice in my life, but shore seems fittin' to me." Peter elbowed Matt. "Won't even mention April's daddy pushed the ox into that ditch."

Tobias, April, and Peter all sauntered off. Kate stooped down to gather the quilt they'd been sitting on.

"Miss Kate, I'll help you shake that out."

"Thanks." They held the corners and flapped the colorful quilt in the slight breeze. Bits of grass fluttered away. Matt looked across the quilt and coordinated folding the ends together and folding the quilt again lengthwise.

"Things went better than I expected with Youngblood," Matt said as he approached her. Kate took the corners, and he bent to lift the fold to double the quilt again.

"I guess it doesn't say much about my faith in my fellow man or in God, but I was sure Mr. Youngblood planned to get ugly."

"I don't have any room to talk." Matt folded his arms

across his chest. "I thought the same thing. He took me by surprise." The corners of his mouth lifted. "So I'll see you at lunch?"

A thrill shot through her. Kate nodded.

"Just a word of advice: a couple of the MacPhersons gigged for frogs last night."

"Cold frog legs?"

"That, too." Matt lowered his voice. "The women saved the skins and were rolling bacon and grits into them today."

Giggles spilled out of her. Matt looked at her as if she'd lost her mind, so she tried to control herself long enough to say, "A special dish like that ought to be reserved for the engaged couples, don't you think?"

"Absolutely."

"What's so funny over there?" April called.

"We were both saying how wonderful it is, knowing how much you and Peter love one another and that you're going to be married."

"Johnna and Trevor, too," Matt tacked on.

❧

"We got us a tradition," Peter's father announced to the crowd as he opened the door to the just-finished cabin. "Started back when Hezzie, Mike, and me got those pretty brides of ourn. Onc't the cabin's done, the groom takes one last gander 'round the inside; then he don't get to see it again 'til his bride's fixed the house into a home."

"The first thing I'm going to do," April said in a merry tone, "is hang curtains so Peter can't peek!"

Peter chuckled and beckoned her.

Uncle Gideon grabbed her. "Young man, the day my daughter becomes your wife, you can carry her over the threshold. Until then, she's mine!"

"Honey pie, how long is it gonna take you to get ever'thang ready?"

"Until Thanksgiving," Johnna declared. "Me and April decided 'twould be fun to have us a double weddin'."

Kate clapped with everyone else, but her joy for her cousin was tinged with sadness. After the Chance clan held a double wedding last year for Laurel and Gabe and Caleb and Greta, Kate had secretly thought it would be lovely if she and April would be able to do the same thing.

"Folks, thar's still gracious plenty on that steer and on the tables." Aunt Lois wiped her hands on the hem of her apron. "Take a look at what all yore hard work got done, then amble on back and fill yore bellies."

Kate waited until most of the others had gone in the front door and exited the back before she stepped onto the porch. Mr. Dorsey unexpectedly turned around and bumped into her. Someone caught her before she fell.

"Whoa. Are you all right, Miss Kate?" Matt set her down and gazed at her with steady brown eyes.

"I'm fine. Just clumsy, that's all."

"It was my fault." Mr. Dorsey gave her an apologetic smile. "I'd say I was weak from lack of food, but you'd laugh me clean out of town. I can't believe Lois thinks any of us can stuff in even one more bite."

"I'm never too full for good chow." Matt grinned. "As soon as we've gone through the cabin, I aim to pile enough food on my plate to feed a bear for winter."

"One plate isn't enough," Kate told him.

"Good thing no one here minds if I go back for seconds."

April ran up and gave Kate a hug. "I can't think of a better place to ask you. I want you by my side at the wedding. You'll be my maid of honor, won't you?"

Birdie tugged on Kate's skirt. "Tell her no. 'Tisn't a good thing, being the old maid. You lose the game on account of bein' the last one."

The last one. That's me.

Matt chortled softly. "Birdie, there's a difference. Old Maid is a card game. Being the maid of honor is a special job."

"But she still don't getta be the married one."

"Not this time," April said.

"But," Matt said as he leaned down and whispered very loudly, "everybody knows the best is always last because she's worth waiting for!"

Kate's heart skipped a beat, then soared. *I've been hoping he felt something for me, Lord. You know how I've tried not to throw myself at him. Thank You for the way Matt seems to understand me and how he says what my heart needs to hear.*

They walked through the cabin, and Kate commented as they exited the back door, "I know they said it's exactly the same as the cabin we share, April, but without anything inside, it feels so big and empty."

"Doesn't it? I already have some ideas. Let's talk over some plans tonight."

"Okay." Kate turned toward Matt. "Ready to eat?"

"Always."

Mrs. White came over. "Oh, dear. Mr. Salter, I feel terrible. Just terrible. You gave me that letter to mail for you, and it's not in my pocket anymore. I've asked everyone to look for it."

"I'm sure it'll turn up."

"But I've never misplaced a single piece of mail. This is—"

"A minor mishap," he soothed. "If we can't find it, I'll write a replacement letter."

"I found it!" One of the Greene's boys ran up and skidded to a dusty stop. "I found it."

"Thanks." Matt accepted the letter and handed it to Mrs. White. "See? Things worked out fine."

Kate felt anything but fine. Her throat constricted, and it hurt to breathe. She could only see part of the address, but even that was too much. Matt was sending a letter to a Miss Jenny Something-or-other.

seventeen

Kate went so white, every last freckle stood out in stark relief. Matt braced her arm. "Miss Kate, are you okay?"

Her head nodded woodenly.

April and he traded concerned looks. "Why don't you sit down here with your cousin? I'll go grab a cup of lemonade for you."

"No. I'm fine. Really. Excuse me." Kate headed off toward the trees.

"I don't like how she looked. No, I don't." Mrs. White made a shooing motion. "April, go on after your cousin, and make sure she's all right."

The envelope in her hand crackled with the action. Matt noticed the address on it. *Kate thinks I'm stringing her along when I already have a sweetheart!* He turned to April, "Miss April, today's a special day for you and Peter. Go on and enjoy yourself. I'll fetch Kate and bring her over so we can all eat a little more of that barbecue."

Matt didn't ask to be excused or wait for a response. He hiked to the edge of the wooded area where Kate had fled. *I have to find her. I can't let a silly misunderstanding come between us. I won't.* Following her didn't take much skill. At first, she'd stayed on the path, but then she'd struck out into an unmarked area. He'd done a fair amount of tracking in the past, and she'd been upset enough to leave a trail. She'd headed deeper into the woods than was wise—a mark of how upset she was. He followed the path she'd left behind and rounded a big pine.

Kate stood in a small clearing and held up a dandelion. Pursing her lips, she gently blew, sending all of the minuscule pieces of fluff into a flurry in the air.

I love her. How could I have done this? I've hurt the woman I love. Those two realizations hit with a double punch. Matt stood there, suddenly aware of just how deeply his feelings ran and what he stood to lose.

"Kate—"

She startled. "What are you doing here?"

"I came to talk with you."

"I'd rather be alone."

Matt approached her slowly. When he got closer, he bent and picked another dandelion. "When I was a boy, my mother said these were like candles on a birthday cake. If you blow it all gone in a single breath, your wish is supposed to come true."

"The nonsense of youth."

"It's not nonsense at all. There's nothing wrong with wishes and dreams." He blew the fluff off his stalk. "See? Now I'm entitled to hope my wish comes true. Know what I was wishing?"

"I'd rather not. I need to get back."

"Kate, I was hoping you'd give me a moment. That letter is going to the lady who ran a boardinghouse I stayed at. She's—"

"It's none of my business." She looked poised to bolt.

He hurriedly said, "Miss Jenny is at least twice my age and reads dime novels. She's worried nefarious bandits are going to bushwhack me, so I promised I'd drop her a line now and then so she wouldn't worry."

"You don't owe me an explanation."

"I might not owe you one, but I want to. Kate, I know we've only recently met, but you're unlike any woman I've ever known."

"I'm different." Her lips twisted wryly. "Yes. I know."

"You're wonderful. Intriguing. Clever and fun to be around." *It's too soon to tell her I love her.* "I hoped maybe you were feeling as comfortable with me as I felt with you."

She compressed her lips and turned away.

"I wouldn't hurt you for anything. You have to trust me on that. Trust your heart, too." He waited as seconds stretched in silence.

Finally, Kate said in a tentative voice, "Nefarious bandits?"

"That's a direct quote. On my wildest day, I couldn't concoct such a phrase. I didn't have the audacity to ask Miss Jenny if there was any other kind of bandit. It might make her self-conscious, and then she'd give up those novels she relishes so much."

"My little brothers and cousins are enamored of Deadwood Dick. If you say anything bad about those novels, the boys might gang up on you."

"Ah. There." He eased one step closer. "See? I blew on the dandelion, and my wish came true. Not only did you stay and hear me out, but you even gave me one of your pretty smiles."

"That's nonsense, and you know it."

"I'll tell you what I know. You're a beautiful young woman. We're alone in the woods, and your daddy's very protective. If I aim to keep life and limb, I'd best escort you out of here and over to the tables."

"I'm not hungry."

"Not even for something small?"

She hitched her shoulder. "It would have to be really little."

"I have just the thing in mind: Eunice's frog-skin-and-grits roll."

Kate's laughter let him know things between them were settled. Matt reached over and took her hand. "Come on. You got pretty far off the path. I don't want you to get lost."

"What path?" She shook her head. "It's gone by now."

"What do you mean?"

"Halfway through these woods, the land changes hands. When the Phillips lived on the other side, they didn't bother to fence in this part of the property. The MacPherson kids would cut through as a shortcut to school."

"But they don't anymore?"

Kate shook her head as he led her.

"Who lives there now?"

"The Youngbloods. He put up a barbed wired fence so he'd keep his cattle out of the MacPhersons' crops. Most folks would split the cost, but Mr. Youngblood paid for it. He said that arrangement was only fair since it made the kids take a longer route."

"Seems mighty generous."

"Unh-huh. Sometimes he comes off as standoffish or gruff, but he's also done some kind things—like apologizing to Peter and sending a couple of workmen."

"Careful. Log's rotten." Matt turned loose of her hand and lifted her over the log.

"This isn't the way I came in." Her gaze darted around.

"The MacPherson kids aren't the only ones who like shortcuts." He kept a light tone, but Matt wanted Kate out of those woods as fast as possible. The path wasn't overgrown as it ought to have been after a few years of neglect. Someone was using it regularly, and he aimed to find out who.

❧

Matt silently entered the cabin and sneaked back into bed. He wouldn't be able to sleep, but he could use the time to formulate a plan.

"You wanna tell us where you've been?" Peter lit a lantern. His father and uncles all glowered at him.

Sitting up slowly, Matt realized he didn't have time to

concoct a plan. He stared at the MacPherson men. "I've been in the woods."

"Ain't the onliest place you've been. Ever' night you've been here, you've snuck out." Peter raised his chin. "I might be plainspoken, but I ain't dumb."

"No one could ever mistake you for being dumb. Yes, I've gone out every night."

Obie's eyes narrowed, and he leaned forward. "You ain't meetin' a gal, are you?"

"No." Matt decided these men were honest. He'd have to trust them. Even warn them. "Someone's been making bootleg whiskey."

Mike nodded. "Yup. That'd be the Youngbloods."

"You knew?" Matt gawked at him.

Mike's brothers sat on either side of him. Their heads cranked toward him, and they said in unison, "How come you didn't tell us?"

"Tempy."

Matt reeled from that reply. "Your wife is involved?"

"Course not!" Mike shook his head. "Tempy's real name— 'tis Temperance on account of her ma namin' all her daughters after the fruits of the Spirit. But her ma skipped a few names and stuck my beloved with that handle as a message to her man. Old man Linden had a still. I didn't want nobody upsettin' Tempy by rakin' up sommat painful in her past."

"You coulda told us. We woulda put a stop to it!"

"Hezzie, you and Obie couldn't keep a secret if your lives depended on it." Mike tapped his boot on the floor.

"So yore the excise man," Hezzie said.

"Not exactly. I've been working as a deputy in San Francisco. Moonshine's been a huge problem, and we've had folks die or go blind from bad batches. I was assigned to locate and shut down the still."

"Niver knowed a deputy who could down trees worth a hoot," Peter's father mumbled.

"You niver knowed a deputy at all," Obie shot back.

Peter ignored them. He stared at Matt. "We're going to put an end to that still. Once we do, you're going to have to reckon with us."

"The Chances, too." Hezzie shook his grizzled head. "I seen their lil' Kate a-lookin' up at you like you done hung the moon. They ain't gonna be happy one bit 'bout how you've played them false."

Matt stood. "Keep Kate out of this."

"Cain't." Obie rose. "We's a-gonna holp you shut down Youngblood's moonshine still, but we ain't a-gonna stand for you breakin' her heart. That gal's like a daughter to us."

❧

Between the MacPherson men and the Chance men, Matt had more than enough help to take Youngblood into custody and dismantle the still. The men all worked together well, carrying the mission with grim determination and near silence. By morning, however, there was no jubilation over their success. Tobias made the discovery that Lucinda was just as deeply involved as her father. That alone was enough to leave the men subdued—but Matt knew the problem ran even deeper than that.

"We don't have a jail. I'll go send a telegram," Caleb said.

"Send it to Sheriff Laumeister in San Francisco." Matt scanned the men. "I've worked alongside you, but it was under false pretenses. When I came here, we didn't know who was involved."

"Don't bother," Kate's father ground out. "You had a job to do, and you did it. That much, we understand. You messed with my little girl, though."

"I didn't plan on falling in love." He stared her father in the eye. "I didn't mess with Kate's heart. She's a special woman, and as soon as I get this matter wrapped up, I aim to come back and court her."

"No, you're not." Her father's declaration would have been easier to take if he'd roared it. Instead, he'd said the words in a low growl.

"Thinking you've found the person God has for you, then discovering they're not what they seem—" Tobias broke off and shook his head. "No. There's no fixing that. You stay away from my sister."

eighteen

"I don't know what to say to her," April said to Peter as they walked along the stream. "Kate's barely talking to any of us. When we came home the night of the cabin raising, she was so excited. Matt had confessed he cared for her."

"For what it's worth, I thank he was tellin' her the truth. When her pa and brother tole Matt to stay 'way from Kate, Matt looked lower'n a snake's belly in a wagon rut."

"You know how much I love you."

"Sure do, honey pie."

"It's hard, though, for Johnna and me to work on our wedding dresses right there in the cabin under Kate's nose. She tries to paste on a smile and even helped baste the skirts, but she's hurting."

"That's gotta be tough. Johnna said Kate's taken it hard. Tobias don't look any better. Him breakin' thangs off with Lucinda—'twasn't an easy decision. But findin' out she was up to her eyebrows in brewin' whiskey—that shook him bad."

"Aunt Lovejoy! It's so nice to see you out here."

"'Tis always a joy to bask in God's sunshine. Makes a body feel all warm and right inside and out." Lovejoy's gaze went from April to Peter and back. "But I look at the both of you's, and neither one of you's wearin' a smile."

April sat next to her aunt on the bench Uncle Dan built for Lovejoy back when he was courting her. "I don't know what to do about Kate," April confessed.

"I reckoned this would come up. A wound niver heals when it's left to fester. Ever'body's tippytoin' 'round and pretendin' nothin's amiss. That's gotta come to an end. Ain't no reason she' cain't have herself a good stormy cry, jist like there's no call for the both of you to be robbed of the joy you ought to be sharin' in yore sweetheart days."

Peter nodded.

"Peter, fetch me a little rock from the crick." He did as she bade, and Lovejoy held the wet pebble and rubbed her thumb over it. Pressing it into April's hand, she said, "That rock weren't smooth a long time back. It had rough edges. God put that rock in the path of water, and that water wore down the sharp spots 'til it turned into a right purdy lil' pebble.

"We cain't say why God sent Matt here. The memory of him's like water, rushing over Kate and wearing her down. Don't know iff'n the dear Lord plans a different man for her—or any man atall, for that matter. Certain as we sit here, God's niver gonna let His children suffer for naught. Someday down the line, we'll look back and see how He directed the currents of life. We all love Kate and wanna protect her from the pain, but if we take her outta the river, then we remove her from where God intended her to be. Iff'n 'twas her life or limb that were at risk, then we'd hop right to it, but when it comes to matters of the heart— well, interfering ain't right. Best thang we cain do is stand 'longside her. Kate's got to trust God that whate'er betides her'll turn out aright as long as she lives in the center of His will."

"That's not just true for Kate." Peter accepted the pebble April handed to him. "It's true for all of us."

"Yup. There ain't no doubt our lovin' heavenly Father wants the both of you to leave and cleave. Don't be so worried o'er something else that you forget what's important: aside from yore relationship with Him, you each gotta be concerned more for one another than anybody else."

"April comes first," Peter declared.

The rapidity and certainty in his response thrilled April. "I feel that way about you, too."

"And God's gonna bless you abundantly. Now go on and moon o'er one another as you finish yore stroll. I aim to be talkin' to the Lord as I sit out here."

"See you later." April gave her aunt a kiss, then placed her hand in Peter's as they started to walk off.

Uncle Daniel came stomping out. "Lovejoy? We've got a problem."

"What's a-wrong?"

"Matthew Salter just took over the Youngblood place and applied to be Reliable's sheriff."

❧

Matt accepted the dipper and gulped down the cool well water. "Thanks, Miss Jenny. How're things looking up at the house?"

"I'm going a room at a time. The two bedrooms were in fine shape, and so were the parlor and kitchen. I can't for the life of me imagine how they allowed the rest of the house to fall into such disrepair!"

"Don't work too hard. We've got nothing but time. Let me know if there's anything else you need." He lifted the pad of paper and started scribbling on it again.

"Salter."

Matt looked up. "Tobias."

"What're you doing here?" Kate's brother didn't bother to dismount.

"I'm setting down roots because I aim to spend my life here."

"Any place else'll do. We don't want you here."

Matt rested his hands on his hips. "I'm not in the least bit surprised."

"Good. Then get—"

"Son." Titus Chance's voice cut through the air. He rode up slowly. In a matter of minutes, so did Kate's uncles, Caleb, and four of the MacPherson men.

Matt stood his ground and said nothing. The verse he'd read that morning in the first chapter of Joshua ran through his mind: *Have not I commanded thee? Be strong and of a good courage; be not afraid, neither be thou dismayed: for the* LORD *thy God is with thee whithersoever thou goest.*

Obie MacPherson called over, "Titus, Kate's yore daughter. Whaddya wanna do 'bout this?"

Kate's dad stared down at him. "Every man's entitled to have a say. You've got one minute, Salter."

"That's more than fair. I did hide my original purpose in coming to Reliable. It's plain to see that gave you cause to distrust me. That's understandable, but you need to know I never told a lie about who I am or how I feel.

"I'm a brother in Christ. Character and integrity matter to me, and that's one of the reasons I became a lawman—to protect the innocent. I appreciate your motive is to protect Kate. I fell in love with her. I make no apologies for any of that, and I'd never knowingly hurt her.

"You told me to keep away from her. I know that's what you want; I don't know if that's what she wants. Kate's an exceptional woman, and God will have to heal the rift between us, but I believe He can. She's worth waiting for.

"I've prayed long and hard. As a result, I'm putting down roots because I'm acting on faith. I want to rear our children here where they'll have grandparents and uncles and aunts and cousins. I'd far rather we all live in harmony."

Silence hovered thick in the air.

"Mr. Salter?" a soft voice called from over by the house.

Obie MacPherson's eyes bulged. "You brung a woman with you!"

Matt elbowed his way past the circle of horses. "Yes, Miss Jenny?"

"You told me to mention anything I need. I can't seem to find a stepladder, and one of the windows in the kitchen is cracked."

"I'll see to those things. Thank you, Miss Jenny."

She began to wring her hands. "I'm sorry I don't have any refreshments ready to offer your friends. If you give me a little time—"

"The gentlemen didn't plan to stay long. Don't worry about that."

Matt watched her until she went back into the house, then he turned back around.

Obie muttered, "I seen buzzards what'd look purdy compared to her."

"Miss Jenny is beautiful on the inside."

"She yore kin?" Hezzie surmised.

"No. She's going to be my housekeeper. I'll definitely hire a cook." Matt gave them a wry look. "You men should thank me for sparing you from eating her food."

"We're taking a vote," Daniel Chance said.

"Us MacPhersons is gonna be in on this here vote," Obie declared.

"The women will have a fit if they find out we didn't include them," one of Kate's uncles said.

"Then we jist won't tell 'em." Peter grinned.

Gideon looked around at the men. "Anyone want to weigh in on the matter before discussion is closed?"

"Yep." Peter pulled a pebble from his pocket. "Dan, yore wife jist gave this to April and me. She's a wise woman."

The men bobbed their heads in silent agreement.

"She said God smooths us with the currents of life. We all love Kate and wanna protect her, but Lovejoy says it ain't right to interfere when 'tis a matter of the heart. We oughtn't to remove Kate from where God intended her to be. Whate'er betides, Kate'll turn out aright as long as she lives in the center of His will. Our place is to stand by her and pray."

"Anyone else?"

Silence.

"Caleb and Tobias are old enough to vote. Peter—"

"If he's old enough to marry my daughter," Gideon said, "he's entitled to vote."

Hezzie scratched his head. "'Zactly what're we votin' on?"

"Cain't make him move." Mike MacPherson mused. "I reckon whether we're gonna let him be near Kate."

"It's not a voting issue. Kate is my daughter." Titus Chance stared down at Matt. "You said some things that bear consideration. In the end, I want my daughter to be happy. Before Peter spoke, I wanted you as far away from my Katie Louise as possible. But that's probably the worst thing that could happen. She has to work through this for herself. I don't want you to go to her, and I'm asking you to give your word that you won't approach her. If she seeks you out, that's her decision."

A wave of relief washed over Matt.

Kate's father continued. "You're on a mighty short rope, Salter. Never thought I'd see the day that one little rock would sway my intent."

"Sir, it's not the size of the rock. We're standing on the Solid Rock together. I wouldn't want to base my life any other way."

nineteen

No matter where she turned, Kate couldn't escape the pain. She went to church, but Matt Salter attended, too. She went to town, and he was walking down the boardwalk, wearing the sheriff's badge. He doffed his hat to her, but then he turned and went the other direction. She wanted to duck into her cabin and be alone, but April and Johnna were there, sewing wedding gowns.

Craving privacy, she went into her workshop. Laying out a tanned skin, she tried to occupy her mind on how best to use the leather.

"Kate?"

"Oh. Hi, Mama."

Her mother pulled out a stool and perched on it. "I've wanted to have some time alone with you. It seems as if everyone's hovering over and crowding you."

"I can hardly breathe."

Mama nodded. "I've tried to give you some time to think matters through. You've always been like that—you need a chance to let everything settle before you make a decision. What are you making?"

"I don't know. I haven't settled on what's the most important thing. I always decide on that before I cut anything out." A rueful laugh bubbled out of her. "At least I'm predictable."

"Matthew Salter has to hold very strong feelings for you, or he wouldn't have come back."

"But how can I trust him? He lied to me."

"Did he lie? From what Caleb and Tobias say, they hired

him to do a fair day's work, and he did more than any hand we've ever had."

"But he deceived me. He acted like he was an ordinary citizen. How can I ever trust that he won't mislead me again?"

"I don't have an answer to that. Have you been praying?"

Kate sniffled and nodded. "I don't have an answer. I keep begging God to show me the way, but He's silent."

"That's a hard place to live. You know we're all praying for you."

"Thank you, Mama."

Mama leaned forward and ran her hand over the leather. "Your Daddy's Bible is about worn through, but he loves it so much, he says he won't use another. Do you think you could make a new cover for it?"

"Sure."

"I thought I heard you in here." Aunt Delilah came in. "I've run out of clothespins, Kate. Do you have more in the basket for me?"

"Yes." Kate went up on tiptoe to reach the pail.

"Good. Laurel sent some pictures for me to take to the gallery. Between her pieces and mine, we'll have enough for a big show."

"Here." Kate set down the bucket.

Aunt Delilah's eyes widened. "I never imagined! With the rest of us gone in Yosemite, I thought the boys would be too busy to whittle much."

Kate leaned over and pretended to examine a spot on the leather.

"Honey," Mama asked, "how did we end up with so many?"

Kate didn't want to answer. She cleared her throat to buy time, but it didn't help. In a tight voice she said, "Matt made a lot of them."

"That was nice of him. I'll have to thank him."

"You don't need to, Aunt Delilah. We didn't tell him about you painting them and giving them away as a thanks to people who sponsor the older orphans' education."

"I take it he doesn't know that our family sponsors the orphanage," Mama said.

"He's aware the family takes wooden toys to the orphanage for Christmas. We've all agreed nobody needs to know you gave that mansion away to be an orphanage, Mama, and the family's support is a case of the left hand not knowing what the right hand is doing."

Dumping the clothespins from the pail into her apron, Aunt Delilah said, "It's okay to keep some things to yourself."

"I know. Those are all things where I wouldn't just be speaking for myself. I'd feel wrong divulging a confidence that I held for others."

Delilah left, and Mama quietly slipped away to get Daddy's Bible. When she came back, she didn't say a word. She set it down on the workbench and walked back out.

Lifting Daddy's Bible, Kate felt the cover on it shift ominously. It was so precarious. *If I make a new cover, maybe we can take this to a bindery in San Francisco and have them repair it. He'd have to make do without it for a while, but in the end, he'll have something that'll last his lifetime.*

Try as she might, Kate couldn't remember the measurements she took so she could cut the leather. After the third time, she grew exasperated with herself. *What's wrong with me?*

She stared at the Bible, then at the clothespin pail. *I feel just as empty as that pail, Lord. What am I going to do?*

Suddenly, I feel guilty. Like I did something wrong. But I didn't. Aunt Delilah even said it was okay to keep some secrets. She leafed through the Bible. It opened to Luke—which came as no surprise. That was Daddy's favorite book of the Bible. Christ's words jumped out at her: "And why beholdest thou the mote that is in thy brother's eye, but perceivest not the beam that is in thine own eye?"

Conviction poured through her. *I felt justified in keeping information back; how can I fault Matt for doing the same thing?*

She tore off her apron and rushed to the stable. The few minutes it took to saddle her mustang felt like an eternity.

"What's got into you?" Tobias asked.

"The truth. I'll be back later."

"Where are you going?"

"Pray for me. I'm hoping to meet my future."

❧

"Sheriff?"

Matt set aside the WANTED posters he'd been studying and rose. "Yes, Mrs. Walcott?"

"Could you please come over to the office?"

The doctor's wife looked a tad flushed and held her baby tight to her bosom. Matt nodded and took his hat off the peg behind his desk. "Is there a problem?"

"Yes, but I think you'll be able to solve it. I think it would be best if I take Ginny Mae and wait over at White's Mercantile."

"Is your husband at risk?"

"No. But please go over and straight into his exam room. You're the only one who can handle this, so you're expected."

Matt figured she'd said as much as she could. He'd learned Polly was a healer, and she and Doc were laudably closed-mouthed about their patients. He headed down the boardwalk with ground-eating strides, considering all of the possible situations he might encounter.

Dr. Walcott's place smelled of lye soap and carbolic acid.

Matt veered to the left as soon as he entered and pushed his way through the curtain.

"Kate!"

She stood on the opposite side of the exam table. "I didn't know where to find you. Your housekeeper thought you might be in town. I didn't want to interrupt if you were in the middle of something important, so I asked Polly to see if you were available."

She'd said all of that in one breath. Matt knew because he hadn't taken a breath, either.

"I was upset because you said you cared, but you kept a big secret from me."

"I know. I'm sorry—"

She held up one hand. "But I had no room to judge. I'd been keeping secrets from you, too. Aunt Delilah and my cousin Laurel are very successful artists. Each Christmas, they paint clothespin ornaments and give a dozen as a thank you to each sponsor who funds the education of one of the older kids at the orphanage. And the orphanage—the one you've mentioned. Mama inherited that mansion. She gave it up to become the new location because the old orphanage was falling apart. And my family—we don't want folks to know that we fund the orphanage."

Matt rounded the table. "Why are you telling me these things?"

"Because I don't ever want dishonesty between us." Tears filled her eyes.

"I don't want that, either." He slowly took her hand in his. "But with my kind of job, there are bound to be times when I can't tell you what's going on."

"I know. I understand now."

"If it'll bother you, I'll give it up in an instant. I bought the

Youngblood place. I could farm or ranch."

"Between the Chances and MacPhersons, there are plenty of those already. They'd gladly rent the land from you."

Matt shook his head slowly. "No, Kate. That's not really what I hoped for."

A stricken look flashed across her face.

He slowly trailed a fingertip across the freckles on her cheek. "I told you that night we did dishes together that I reckoned the only woman I'd call simply by her given name would be my wife. That day I sought you out in the woods, you might not have noticed, but I stopped calling you Miss Kate. I did that because I realized I'd fallen in love with you and wanted you to be mine. What I've been hoping for, praying for, was to have you as my wife."

At first, she gaped. Then the very tip of her tongue slipped out to moisten her lips.

"I'm not the most patient man, but I'll wait until you figure out your feelings. I know where I stand, and if it takes seven years to court you, I'll do it, just like Jacob waited for Rachel in the Bible."

"It took him fourteen years." Her voice sounded low and shaky.

That reminder didn't please him, but Matt tamped down his feelings. Kate's feelings were what counted. "If it takes twice that long, I'll wait. I love you, Kate. Nothing's going to change that."

"I love you, too."

Her admission nearly knocked him out of his boots.

"But Matt?"

"Yes?"

"There's a problem."

"Darlin', nothing is going to stand in our way. Look how

far God's brought us."

"I met Miss Jenny. She insisted on giving me a cookie and a glass of lemonade. She's a nice lady, but we'll both be seeing God a lot sooner than we imagined if we keep her as our cook."

epilogue

Folks packed the pews in church. Johnna squeezed April tight. "'Tis a joy to be sharin' today, ain't it?"

"Yes!" April then whispered, "Kate told me Miss Jenny made potato salad."

"Thanks for warnin' me. Last thang I want is to wind up ailin' from our weddin' supper. I s'pose I ought to mention that you'll want to thank Aunt Eunice for doing sommat special. She took a mind to fancify the deviled eggs. They're a right purdy color on account of her addin' Tabasco to the yolks."

"I'll be sure to pass the word on."

"You gals best save your talkin' for the words what matter most down at the altar," Uncle Obie said.

Tobias and Caleb opened the doors from the narthex to the sanctuary, and the organist began to play the "Wedding March." Johnna held her father's arm and a sheaf of yellow roses as she walked down the aisle.

Trevor could barely wait for her. Uncle Obie's normally booming voice had a catch to it when he said, "I ain't a-gonna give up my little girl 'til she give me one last kiss."

Johnna calmly handed her roses to Trevor, lifted her veil, and bussed her pa.

"Ain't easy. I'm marryin' off my two eldest today. But Trevor, ain't a better man for my Johnna, so I'm a-givin' her to you."

Trevor handed back Johnna's flowers. "I'll love her forever."

"I aim to go sit by my Lois so's we cain share the sight of my son's bride a-walking down this aisle." Uncle Obie tugged

Lois out into the aisle, stepped in, and tugged her to his side. "You cain't see past me, sugar. Here you are."

The organist took her cue and began playing again. Gideon Chance stood in front of April, blocking everyone's view of her. He lit the white pillar candle she held. "You're beautiful, sweetheart. Mama and I love you and trust God to bless you and Peter."

"I love you, too, Daddy." She peeked around him as Peter stepped to the front of the church. April let out a delighted laugh. "Oh, Daddy—I asked him not to wear a white shirt, and he didn't! The only thing more golden than that shirt is his heart."

Gideon Chance stepped to the side, and April slid her hand into the crook of his elbow. Joy lit Peter's face as soon as he saw his bride.

Tobias continued to hold the door open and looked at Kate. "Take off those gloves, sis. Matt loves you just as you are."

Kate hastily tugged off the gloves, and Tobias shoved them into his pocket. Her father smiled as he pressed his newly covered Bible into her hands. "You look just as pretty as your mama did in that gown, Katie."

"Thank you, Daddy."

"Dad," Tobias hissed. "The music's started up again. Get going!"

Titus Chance shot his eldest a reproving look. "Salter knows my daughter is worth waiting for."

"He's patient, Daddy," Kate agreed. "But I'm not. If you don't give me your arm, I'm going to gallop down the aisle all by myself."

He threaded her arm through his and chuckled. "You'll always be my little girl."

"Yes, Daddy, I will." Kate looked ahead at her bridegroom. "But even more, I'll be Matt's wife."

All three couples stood at the altar. Pastor Abe smiled at them. "God's home is always full of hope and love. Today, an extra measure of both has been poured out upon us because three of our young couples are here to pledge their hearts in holy matrimony."

Sacred vows were exchanged, communion was shared, then each couple sealed their promises with a kiss.

The pastor looked at Johnna and Trevor, then April and Peter, and finally at Kate and Matt. "It's my privilege to pronounce these three couples as man and wife. Surely we can all say our cup runneth over with love."

A Letter To Our Readers

Dear Reader:

In order that we might better contribute to your reading enjoyment, we would appreciate your taking a few minutes to respond to the following questions. We welcome your comments and read each form and letter we receive. When completed, please return to the following:

Fiction Editor
Heartsong Presents
PO Box 719
Uhrichsville, Ohio 44683

1. Did you enjoy reading *No Buttons or Beaux* by Cathy Marie Hake?
   ❑ Very much! I would like to see more books by this author!
   ❑ Moderately. I would have enjoyed it more if

   _____
   _____
   _____

2. Are you a member of **Heartsong Presents**? ❑ Yes ❑ No
   If no, where did you purchase this book? _____
   _____

3. How would you rate, on a scale from 1 (poor) to 5 (superior), the cover design? _____

4. On a scale from 1 (poor) to 10 (superior), please rate the following elements.

   ____ Heroine   ____ Plot
   ____ Hero   ____ Inspirational theme
   ____ Setting   ____ Secondary characters

5. These characters were special because? _____

_____

_____

6. How has this book inspired your life? _____

_____

_____

7. What settings would you like to see covered in future **Heartsong Presents** books? _____

_____

_____

8. What are some inspirational themes you would like to see treated in future books? _____

_____

_____

9. Would you be interested in reading other **Heartsong Presents** titles? ❏ Yes ❏ No

10. Please check your age range:

    ❏ Under 18   ❏ 18-24

    ❏ 25-34   ❏ 35-45

    ❏ 46-55   ❏ Over 55

Name _____

Occupation _____

Address _____

City, State, Zip_____

Heart♥ng

─── **Presents** ───